Princess of the Night Rides

Princess of the Night Rides
and Other Tales

by
John Dominis Holt

Decorations by Marcia Morse

Topgallant Publishing Co., Ltd.
Honolulu, Hawaii
1977

Copyright © 1977 by John Dominis Holt

All rights reserved. No part of this book may be reproduced or transmitted in any form or by any means, electronic or mechanical, including photocopying, recording or by any information storage and retrieval system, without permission in writing from the publisher.

First Printing 1977

Some of the tales in this volume appeared originally in *Today Ees Sad-dy Night and Other Stories,* published December, 1965.

TOPGALLANT PUBLISHING CO., LTD.
845 Mission Lane
Honolulu, Hawaii 96813

Printed in the United States of America

Library of Congress Cataloging in Publication Data

Holt, John Dominis.
   Princess of the night rides and other tales.

   1. Holt, John Dominis—
                             76-12962
ISBN 0–914916–21–1 (cloth)
ISBN 0–914916–22–X (paper)

This book is for my parents.

Table of Contents

"God Sent You Into That Gomorrah This Morning To Bring Up The Truth"   1

The Pool   13

Today Ees Sad-dy Night   23

Princess of the Night Rides   37

Olga Kaupiko's Treasure   61

The Ditchman's Bride   75

"So Long As A Man's Family Continued In Possession Of A Cave"   89

Christmas Eve on Upper Fort Street   101

Family Portraits   107

Johnny Warm   137

Princess of the Night Rides

"God Sent You into That Gomorrah This Morning to Bring up the Truth"

The men had come to capture alligators that were—according to a friend of a friend of the telephone operator at the Forestry Office—thriving in the entanglement of jungle and swamp in our deep gulch.

"Please come in," I offered. "Come in, and sit down! This needs some explanation!"

"There is no need for explanation. We just want the alligators. We've brought fish nets and a couple of guns that we'll use, if it is necessary. You know, of course, that it is illegal to keep alligators in Hawaii?"

"I am perfectly aware of this, and I am afraid you would feel pretty silly if you went down into the gulch with all your gear, only to discover that there are no alligators—no, not one!"

"We've heard from good authority that there *are* alligators here," volunteered the tall thin haole in the group of four men.

They came in now, wearing the gray look of patient suspicion. As logically as I could, I reconstructed the saga of Pauline's alligators: perhaps in not as full detail as this reportage, for I doubt if their patience would have endured some of the more abstract or surmised elements concerning Pauline's bizarre *idee fixe*. However, it is still a puzzle to me how they could have left us with the same sober and patient mien that they wore upon their arrival, after having been convinced, finally, that, perhaps, there were no alligators in Halekoa gulch.

Our property was a large one, substantially covered with tropical growth. Several mango trees—immense, dark, and brooding—occupied a space between the two main dwellings: one, our house; the other, an arrangement for guests. It was past a hundred years since the oval hirsute seeds of mango had been put into the dark island earth by a horticultural-minded ancestor, to grow above ferns and ginger into the giants they had become. In their advanced state of age they had assumed majestical elegance—mammoth sentinels, watching over the life of the murky and wet gulch, a no-man's-land for the children of the family for generations. The large pond, choked in spots with the growth of pink lotus and water lilies of many colors, reflected portions of the forms of one group of the mango trees, a cluster of four growing at the mauka, or upper, end of the property.

Water oozed from a number of unpredictable spots in the basin of the gulch. The area was so lavishly endowed with artesian springs that the two large ponds were never dry. This abundance of water created the perfect environment for the growth of aquaceous plants and should have provided a sumptuous haven for exotic waterfowl, snakes, and other reptilia, had such creatures been extant in the islands of Hawaii.

The gulch also provided a treasure trove of possibilities for the imaginative, the speculatively inclined. Its darkness, the lavish vegetation, its wetness gave to it an aura of the mysterious, promising all sorts of vaporous happenings should one wish to explore the nebulous twistings of growth: hau, guava, Java plum, and miles of maile pilau, that odoriferous and malignant vine which grows with such vigor—such tenacity—in almost every *milieu* of growing condition in the islands. I, myself, had nurtured for years a secret hope that we would someday find a small colony of proboscis monkeys, quietly undergoing existence in one of the darker corners of the area. Usually only the gardeners penetrated the muck and thickened growth of the gulch, venturing into it to cut stalks of bamboo or to collect the massive waxy and powerfully symbolic blossoms of torch ginger.

Sections of the amorphous tangle had been wrested gradually from nature and brought into the orbit of the garden scheme. My grandfather had begun a botanical collection: mainly fruiting trees, bamboo varieties, and water-loving plants. It had assumed a sort of catch-as-catch-can order as his scheme took shape. New paths and stone steps were set along the steep banks of the house side of the gulch. A wide grass passage was kept meticulously groomed around the ponds; and whole areas of the marshy bottom of the gulch began to burst with the growth of numerous ginger varieties, and other stranger plants imported from distant, impossible places—the warm tropical corners of the earth around.

Gradually, one whole side of the gulch had been developed into gardens. Cunning elusive paths meandered through groves of two or so dozen varieties of bamboo, or under the spreading round-leafed canopy of *Macaranga grandifolia*, or through densely massed *Monstera deliciosia*, clinging to the sharp banks. At one section, the paths wandered through a marvelous jungle of *Ravanela*, the traveler's palm of Madagascar, whose massive leaves from a distance suggest the foliage of a giant banana.

Our old friend, Pauline Irwin, could not resist imbuing the gulch with a vast life of mystery, where strange animalia and even strange people might lurk in the dark corners, writhing in living patterns of vicious iniquity. She had imposed an absolute taboo upon the gulch with regard to herself. It was a forbidding and evil territory—a shadowy kingdom to which no decent person should pay homage by the act of submitting his presence to its depths. Certainly, it was no place for a Christian lady. Even the well-kept paths and stairways winding along the steep banks that fell into the rich swampy abyss of the gulch had not gained her respect. It was remarkable, to me, how far Pauline had wandered from the superb empathy her Polynesian forebears had known with earth, sky, and water.

"I swear it is inhabited by all kinds of vicious creatures," she would say; and no one challenged her right to say this, though we all knew the gulch was as safe to travelers as the great lawn that swept across the middle of the thirty acres of gardens that surrounded us at Halekoa.

"I will never go into that horrid place," she was fond of saying. "How can you keep taking guests, especially mainland people, down there. The place must be a regular haven for devils. It must give people some strange ideas about us!"

Or when the gardeners brought armloads of ginger, heliconia, papyrus, or fat stalks of bamboo for use in the house, she would demand, "Wash those things thoroughly!" To Pauline, they did not deserve the name of foliage or flowers, coming as they did from the underworld of the gulch. "They must be covered with vermin!"

"Really, Emma," she would turn to my mother appealingly, "how can you allow *things* to be brought from *down there* into your lovely house?"

"But they are beautiful flowers and greens! And, for the millionth time, Pauline, the gulch is not infested with vermin!"

"Ha! You will see!" and wheezing vigorously, poised for a siege of asthma, she would add, "They will bring up strange things someday, and you people will be sorry you own that gulch."

Thoughts of the dark, verminous place sometimes brought on the frequent attacks of asthma that Pauline had when she came to Halekoa. And it was strange how her physical appearance somehow coincided with her funny little obsessions, like this one regarding our gulch. She was tall, thin, rather dark, and very wraithlike in her movements, due, perhaps, to her asthmatic affliction. She tired easily, and moved about always with slow graceful movements.

We could never determine the true basis for Pauline's horror of the gulch. Although for years—from the age of three until she was seventeen—she had received an Anglicized education at the Priory in Honolulu, she still clung to many Hawaiian superstitions that referred back to the old neolithic culture. She was a mixture of pagan and enlightened Christian beliefs. Her parents, both of part-Hawaiian extraction, were staunch and lifelong members of the Anglican Church of Hawaii as were most of the rich and fashionable people of the Hawaiian community in the days of the monarchy. Yet, like Pauline, they might well have clung, in their day, to certain lingering oddments of thinking based in the beliefs of pre-white Hawaii—much as Pauline did in our times.

In some matters, she was extremely rational, and showed in her general thinking an alertness not common to ladies of her generation and background in Hawaii. She could quote whole passages from Byron's heroic poems and remembered certain lines from Wordsworth, Keats, and the sonnets of Mrs. Browning. She had read some of Thomas Babington Macaulay, and some of Thomas Carlyle, and she could present a fair dissertation on the works of Charlotte and Emily Bronte to any circle of patient listeners. Suitably educated, in the Victorian sense, she exceeded, by far, the literary and musical tastes of most of her contemporaries in the islands of the Earl of Sandwich.

In her younger days, she had been a rather good pianist. I can remember, years back to childhood, listening to Pauline play from the waltzes, nocturnes and etudes of Chopin, using a delicate touch and performing with such feeling one would have to admit that her interpretations were poetic and heart-felt.

Her entire being suggested a delicacy of spirit and refinement. She was stubbornly a *jeune fille* long, long after she had lived beyond the physiological limits allowed this stage in a woman's development.

Only when she poked her mental finger into supernatural "evils," or the more natural manifestations lodged in those healthily-growing specimens of plants in our gulch, did she seem, perhaps, not so innocent and, perhaps, on more familiar terms than is "nice" with "evil." Or was she only, after all, a child being titillated by the fascinating and elusive aspects of corruption.

We had tried for years to understand the basis for some of Pauline's thoughts, attacking the problem individually, or as a group which included members of the family and certain friends. Some of her fancies were charming and had enriched many a family confab. But other of her pet fantasies could be quite disturbing to older more conservative friends.

She saw occult significance in the weather, in the behavior of dogs and cats. She held odd views of certain families, giving them a character suggested by the behavior of ancestors of whom she had only heard and never known. Because of the old grandfather, "the So-and-Sos are pathologically miserly," or "The D's were ghost-ridden, and have been ever since Grandfather D had leaped from the cliffs at Napali"—into a luxuriant valley below.

Then, too, she gave whole nations of people specific physical or emotional attributes, based on the observations she had made of individual representatives with whom she had been in contact, or from something she had read. The English were haughty and austere, tall and stately, built on the prototypes of Wellington, Melbourne, Queen Elizabeth, and the gorgeous ladies of Gainsborough's canvases; but they all suffered from anaemia and certain respiratory diseases. The dumpy plainness of the nuns at the Priory and their superb good health had done nothing to destroy the illusion. The Chinese people, who came from regions bordering the great rivers, had skins that were scaly because of the abundance of a very scaly fish in their diet. The people of India were all thin and bony because their religious beliefs compelled them to sit around in temples all day to fast and smell incense. Nothing cast a nation lower, in Pauline's estimation, than if some of its people burned incense in connection with worship. Combining the inhalation of aromatic essences with spiritual worship bore for Pauline a most obscene connotation.

Houses suffered brutally under Pauline's sensitive urges and responses. Every house in which she had spent any length of time unleashed certain strong emotions in Pauline. Although there would be many details connected with each in her mind they fell into two general categories: the ghostly, and the non-ghostly. Armed with the category into which she placed a particular house, she would extoll or condemn, taking great pains to describe the emotions she had felt at each visit. A house was "clean" if it did not effulge ghostliness; it was lepo, or soiled, if it did. A certain house in Nuuanu, where she had spent weekends with an elderly cousin, was the "Queen's bed's house." There she had slept in a massive, ornate bed, which a Hawaiian Queen had brought from Paris in the 1860's, and was not told its history until the following morning. She lived in horror of her cousin's house ever after. "That awful house of my cousin Kalani, and that awful bed!" Forty years later, she still squirmed with fear, speaking of the house, the bed. In another house, there could be a room, or a passageway, or a door, that contained the supernatural element. "Victoria Arlington's old house is haunted! Maka'u loa ke ia hale! A frightening house! The door leading from the bedroom hall to the living room opens mysteriously at night—even after it has been shut tightly! I saw it happen twice!" Pauline had repeatedly told of her experience in the Arlington house, concerning one of its hall doors.

It had been generally conceded that in the conglomerate of oddities of thinking that filled Pauline's mind, her fear of our gulch at Halekoa was just another oddity, like her insisting the fruit of the *Monstera deliciosa* contained seven distinct flavors miraculously intact in the single fruit: lemon, lime, pineapple, strawberry, orange, banana, and one other which she could never remember.

So, when Cousin Aileen went into the gulch that day, determined to explore every cranny and nook in search of ginger blossoms, papyrus, and water lily blooms, it was natural that Pauline should declare Aileen insane, on the spot:

"Have you lost your mind—to go into that Gomorrah? Why, my dear, it is infested with evil things!"

"I have wanted to explore it for years! It's been such a hotbed of mystery! I've never been down to the other side of the gulch—only on the grass paths. This is my chance! Besides, we need flowers for the New Year's party!"

"I'll buy flowers from the florist for the party!" Pauline offered quickly.

"O, no! You *can't* just *buy* some of the treasures that grow down there. It's like Africa, or the jungles of Brazil—all those choice, imported plants!"

"And they're all poisonous—evil—like so much that is found in Africa and Brazil."

"Really, Pauline," Aileen snorted in exasperation. Then, seizing the moment, she suggested, "Since I'm determined to go down into that gulch, I promise to bring you a detailed account of everything—*everything!*"

"That's fine. I'm going to stand watch at the top of the trail and wait for you to return. If anything happens, you be sure to yell for help. I've been told one's hair can turn white in a moment with fright, and you have such beautiful hair! I would just hate to see it change color now."

Pauline became a little breathless with the anticipation of inevitable disaster. Her bronchi rattled under the impetus. "Really, Aileen, to do this at your age. You ought to be ashamed!" She wheezed and coughed, producing sounds like those made by antiquated gas water-heaters in London.

"I've told you a thousand times, we've all told you, there is nothing to be afraid of in that gulch. Nothing!" My mother had come upon the scene, and, overhearing Pauline's last dire remarks, she had felt compelled to make again the statement of reassurance she had made hundreds of times before. "It's absolutely safe, Pauline! Absolutely!"

"That's what you think, Emma Newton! *I* lived in this valley as a young girl with my old uncle and his wife—for many a summer! You know, Uncle Henry, he could tell, you remember, if the telephone rang at certain times—even before answering it—that it would be a call telling us that someone had died. Well, he ordered us to keep strictly away from this gulch. *You* only came here after you were married. You don't know the true history of this place!" Then, as if she were struck by a divine power with profoundly revealing insight, she said softly, but emphatically, "Why, do you know, there is even a bed of quicksand in that gulch!"

In all the years—the centuries of man's inhabiting of the Hawaiian Archipelago—there is no evidence that anyone has ever discovered the existence of such sand, *anywhere*, on any of the islands that comprise the chain. Mud? Yes. Sand? Yes. But quicksand?

My mother went about her business, leaving Pauline to her odd prognostications and Aileen to her foraging. So many times she had patiently attempted to divest Pauline Irwin of some of her untenable fancies, fearing that someday they would lead her, willy-nilly, into madness; but Pauline stubbornly kept the lurid impaled on some cornice of her mind. It had become a part of the fabric of her awareness at all times. She lived for the noble purpose of surviving the fearful. Life was an endless concatenate of bizarre threats from the world of the occult. To live was largely a matter of meeting the challenge of these threats; it was a fixed element of one's sense of responsibility.

She believed that hairy children—part ape, part human—inhabited the jungles of Sumatra. Somewhere, she had read, and believed, an account of mermaids being seen off the coast of Patagonia; and, years before, an aging British countess, who had passed through Hawaii after an exploring trip through Australia, had mentioned to Pauline the possibility of Paleozoic monsters being still extant in the vast interior of that distant continent. After being given this fascinating morsel of intelligence, Pauline suffered perserverating thoughts in which a giant beast kept dipping its vast head into slimy water, bringing up stringy bunches of seaweed after each thrust—a clear-cut image, exceeding the chimaera impressionism of a dream.

And, yes, there were sea monsters, and werewolves; and every phony charlatanic story resulting from the excavation of Tutankhamen's tomb Pauline accepted as the truth, *carte blanche*. She was an encyclopaedia of information of the sort which endlessly filled the pages of the *American Weekly* for a generation, or so, in the late Victorian times.

But for us, the most absurd of Pauline's soaring fantasies was her belief that there were alligators in the gulch at Halekoa. For years she had mentioned, always rather furtively, the possibility of this being so. Her obsession had begun from something her great-aunt had told her when Pauline was a little girl and would come to visit her relatives in the valley of Halekoa. The old woman had whispered something to the effect that my great-grandfather had brought giant lizards from somewhere in the Orient and had planted them in the gulch of his property which lay across the street from theirs.

Roaming, adventurous Englishmen were specialists in collecting exotica. Some of the old alii, Hawaiian nobility, who had traveled to England had returned to Hawaii, telling of the odd collections of plants and animals they had seen at the estates of the great lords whom they visited. After years of attempting to discourage Pauline in this belief that my grandfather had planted alligators in his gulch, members of the family circle tacitly agreed to allow her the fiction. My cousin, Aileen Ragsdale, in later years had remarked, "It's a wonder she hasn't carried this gruesome illusion outside the family." Oddly enough, she had not.

And then, on this day preceding our annual New Year's party, Aileen set out upon her venture of flower gathering in the gulch, taking two of the gardeners as a sort of gunbearer and his assistant *entourage!* Pauline had insisted that Aileen not go unprotected on this safari. Carrying *machetes,* pruning shears, and sharp sickles—all implements useful in gathering up the kind of tropical bloomage Aileen was so determined to collect—the little caravan made its descent into the dark marsh.

"Please take good care of yourself, my dear," Pauline had called out wistfully. "And remember, if anything happens, you must call for my help."

She envisioned the gaping, dripping jaws of a massive reptile, lying hidden in the ooze of the lower pond, poised for a quick attack upon Aileen: an image which flushed up in her mind the memory of what the peeress of Britain had told her of prehistoric creatures roaming the interior of the Australian continent.

But Aileen's venture into the gulch this morning was in keeping with her background. It was in line with the bizarre and radical antics of some of her forefathers. And the fact that my family should maintain such a property as the gulch kept intact the purity of idiosyncratic tendency, so far as we, the Newtons, were concerned. We were strange creatures, all!

I could walk the trails, and oversee care of the extensive plantings of exotic luxuriant moisture-loving vegetation, without evincing more than a small statement of caution from Pauline. I was young and strong and could resist any lurking dangers. Besides, it was my duty! Anyway, I was male; and, being so, a little of original sin lurked, also, in me.

We were curious families: the Archers and my family, the Newtons. All kinds of funny people were in both families, and now they had been joined again, for the first time in sixty years, with the marriage of my sister Cordelia to Aileen Archer Ragsdale's eldest son Archer Ragsdale. Pauline had heard, most of her life, of the antics of the old governor, Aileen's grandfather, and various other Archer antecedents. Then, too, there was all the talk of my great uncles; especially Uncle Timothy Newton, who had lost an eye brawling in some tavern when he was a young boy at school, which necessitated forever after his wearing a black eye-patch.

Pauline shivered when she thought of the old Newton ranch at Mikilua: the strange menagerie that had collected there, of monkeys, peacocks, macaws, and what had seemed to her to be an army of vicious dogs. She had visited the ranch only twice, as the guest of my great aunts, who had been her classmates at the Priory school. Her memory of the sprawling house, its huge rooms, and the great trees which surrounded that structure was filled with almost hysterical terror.

But Aileen Archer's gesture on that morning, as she descended into the gulch, provided a *coup de grace*. Bolstered by her reminiscences, Pauline Irwin could stand at the top of the trail and weave the pattern of attributes characterizing the Archer and Newton families. There was no other way to release the annoyance. These annoying attributes related comfortably to the rest of the legendary myths that saturated her mind.

If the gulch was possessed of evil, and Satan sat over it all, it was only natural for Pauline to see an element of satanic verisimilitude in Aileen's act; or, so far as we were concerned, in the raw cruel fact that we should want to continue to own the property of which the gulch was so intrinsic a part. The thoughts occurred to her again, and again; and her mind, like a great sponge, soaked up images which they had released. These occurred with such vehemence, with such divinely instigated force, that she was helpless to suppress any of the unflattering attributes of character which this imagery cast upon the Archer and Newton families.

She plucked a fragment of laua'e fern and brought it to her nose. Its sweet fragrance soothed her briefly. The olfactory stimulus diverted her thoughts temporarily away from speculations regarding the peculiarities of the two families. "They are very peculiar people—of one stripe, they are!" Helpless, again, to effect any further restraints of her thoughts, Pauline gave in to the urge to dwell further upon the Archer and Newton oddities of behavior.

She thought of Aileen's Grandfather Archer's famous gardens in Waikiki. She had been there a number of times before the old house was torn down and its ponds drained off. Her ears, in remembering Ua-hania, were filled with the eerie screechings of peacocks and her vision crowded with the shadows cast upon the ground by the swaying branches of enormous India banyan trees. Automatically struck by their resemblance in size to the trees she remembered at Ua-hania, she looked into the great old mango trees above her. How dark and brooding they were!

"Evil things! They should be cut down!" she thought. "Or at least thinned out!"

She started to count the aged fruit trees, then stopped. Somewhere from the recesses of her mind, a thought leaped out, telling her that it was bad luck to count. Bad luck to count . . . "Aileen," she called out. "Are you all right?" There was no answer.

Then, with a force to equal loud peals of thunder, flashing of lightning, and the cruel push of rushing waters, her thoughts shaped into a new design:

Today she would know! Aileen would tell her the truth. She was a very straightforward woman. She would know, for a fact, today, if there were alligators in that loathsome gulch. And if there were alligators in the gulch of Halekoa, it would be the final triumph of her having faithfully kept this macabre truth dancing on the fringes of her mind for all these years.

When Aileen returned, at last, weighted down by armloads of ginger and heliconia, she presented a picture of bucolic excellence.

The gardeners who had accompanied her followed, carrying stalks of papyrus, and a number of huge lotus blossoms, and pads that would dry fast and wrinkle up into fascinating clusters.

"Thank God, you're safe, Aileen! I was worried sick!"

Pauline had stood watch at the head of the trail for more than an hour. She quivered with hope for the report verifying her precious knowledge of one kind of the gulch's inhabitants.

Aileen, muddy and wet all over, put down her waxy surrealist burden. "I left my cigarettes here, someplace." She rustled her hands searchingly through some of the laua'e fern leaves.

"No, they are here." Pauline pointed to a moss-covered rock. "I picked them up and put them there."

Aileen recovered the cigarettes, took one slowly from the package, tamped one end of it on her thumb, and then, with further deliberation and what seemed to Pauline needless ceremony, placed it between her lips and lighted up. The whole act, although not taking more than a brief minute of time to accomplish, seemed to Pauline to consume an hour.

"Tell me, for God's sake, tell me! What did you see?"

Aileen inhaled a deep draw of smoke, and blew it out slowly. She asked a gardener to take the flowers to the house. When he had gone, she turned to Pauline, took another draw on her cigarette, and, after exhaling the smoke, said, "I saw an alligator. In fact, I saw two. One was on the trail, the other in one of the pools."

Praise God from whom all blessings flow! Here was verification! Her old tutu had told the truth! "Aileen, how marvelous! I mean, how horrible! But tell me—the one on the trail—did you touch it?"

"I certainly did! It was only about three feet long. I turned it over with this stick!" She pointed to a stick she had cast aside when she had searched for her cigarettes.

Pauline's eyes followed the gesture. Quickly the thoughts came, and the words rushed out: "Tell me, then, tell me, was it a boy, or a girl?"

Aileen, at this point, could barely prevent a telltale smile from shaping on her face. "So far as I could tell, it was a boy! A bouncing sturdy little boy alligator!"

Pauline was near crying; her eyes were moist, but, somehow, there was no evidence of an impending asthmatic attack. In spite of her state of joyous triumph, the affliction had won a temporary respite.

"At last, I know this to be the truth!" Her voice cracked, and she firmed herself within to suppress the tears of triumph. Then she said chokingly, "God sent you into that Gomorrah this morning to bring up the truth! I have always known something evil went on down there—and now, you have come back, having run smack into an alligator. And what, pray tell, could be more evil?" She gave the entangled composite of the gulch, the great mango trees, a vicious leer that was at once reproachful and triumphant.

"Let's hurry back to the house, my dear. I must tell Emma, and, besides, you ought to be getting out of those wet clothes."

The tall haole had sat expressionless as I related the fantasy of Pauline and the alligators. No matter to what lengths of detail and logic I went in an attempt to explain away this strangely-tinged matter, hoping to preserve some dignity for ourselves and the Forestry Office men, they did not accept anything I said by word, smile, grunt, or any other visual or auditory kind of response.

Adventure had been promised—adventure in fulfilling the routine demands of duty—and now—

"I'm sorry you came all the way down here and went through all the trouble of loading your gear."

They rose in a chorus.

At the door, the tall thin haole—he had not offered us his name—stopped short, paused, and said quietly, and very knowingly:

"I have learned, if you ever do run into an alligator, and you want to subdue him, pinch the fleshy section at the side of his jaws—the place where the upper and lower jaws meet. Just take hold of the corner like this,"—he demonstrated by pinching the corner of his own mouth—"and hold on firmly. This immobilizes the alligator."

And, with this parting gift of precious information, he turned away, and walked toward the station wagon where his three silent companions had already found places in which to settle comfortably for the long ride back into Honolulu.

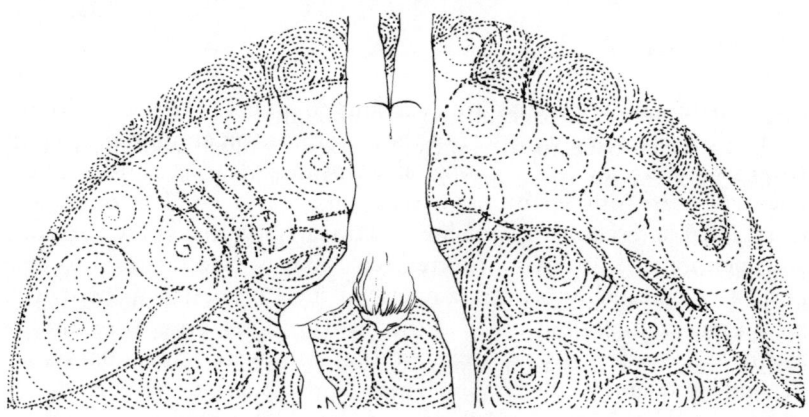

The Pool

It was perhaps as large as a good-sized house. It tended to be round in shape. At the far southern end of Kawela Bay, it sat open to the wind, the sun. Scattered clumps of coconut grew around it, splashing shade with the look of Rorschach ink blots here and there at the edges of the water.

Fresh water fed into it from underground arteries, blended with warmer water pushed in by the tide from the sea through a volcanic umbilical cord. "The lagoon," as we called it, had a definitive link to the sea, being joined as it was by virtue of this unique tubular connection.

We were always afraid of "the lagoon." For one thing it was alleged to be so deep as to be way beyond anyone's imagination—like the idea of endless space to the universe or the unending possibilities of time. Its dark blue-green waters were testament to the fact of the pool being deep according to our elders. We accepted their calculation, but not entirely. It was deep to be sure, but not depthless.

Within "the lagoon," huge ulua, a local variety of pompano or crevalle, would suddenly appear in ravenous groups of three or four, chasing mullet in from the sea. Once in the confines of this small body of water the mullet were no match for the larger, carnivorous predators. Ulua could grow to the size of three or four feet and weigh nearly a hundred pounds. The mullet feasts by ulua in the lagoon were wild and unpleasant scenes. We would watch as children, both enthralled and frightened, as mullet leaped for their lives in glittering silvery schools of forty or fifty fish, some to fall with deadly precision into the jaws of the larger fish. The waters swirled then and sometimes became bloody. The old folks said this would attract sharks. They would wait at the opening of the tube in the ocean to prey on the ulua, whose bellies now were fat from feasting on mullet. These tumultuous invasions were not frequent, but they were reason enough to keep us from swimming in "the lagoon." Perhaps most fearful to us were the tales we heard offered by assorted adults that a goddess of ancient times inhabited these strange blue-green waters. Some knew her name and mentioned it. I have forgotten what it was. She was said to be a creature of unearthly beauty, a queen of the Polynesian spirit world, who revealed herself at times in the forms of great strands of limu, a special seaweed growing only in brackish water; her appearance depending on tides, the moon, winds, and certain cosmic manifestations we could not completely understand because they were mentioned in Hawaiian.

I wandered by the hour in the area of "the lagoon" and on the reefs nearby with an ancient, bearded sage who was our caretaker. His hut of clapboard and corrugated roofing sat near an old kuula, a fisherman's shrine, half-hidden under some hau bushes. His people had been fishermen from time immemorial. Some of his relatives lived a short distance down the coast toward Waimea Bay. Infrequent visits were made upon the old man by these ohana; usually three or four young men came to consult him about fishing. His knowledge of the north shore and its inhabitants in the sea was vast. Once or twice a year he paid a ritual visit to their little house standing in its tiny lawn surrounded by taro patches and sheltered at the front by clumps of coconut and lauhala trees. He spent hours explaining in Hawaiian, and in his own unique use of pidgin, the lore of the region, mentioning with distaste his wine-drinking nephews. I was only four or five years of age at the time. Much of his old-world ramblings is now lost to me.

But I do remember him mentioning that the sea entrance to "the lagoon" was too deep for him to take me to it. He was too old now to dive to those depths. He secretly led me to the kuula, a built-up rock shrine, round in shape, where we took small reef fish and crustacea we had speared. We would pray; the old man in Hawaiian, I in a mixture of the old native tongue and English. It was being impressed upon us now we must speak perfect English. The use of Hawaiian was discouraged. After prayers we would leave offerings on the kuula walls, walk to "the lagoon" where more prayers were said and the remaining bits of fish thrown into the pool as offerings to the beautiful goddess.

All of these activities fell within a definitive framework of time and circumstance. These were not helter-skelter rituals. I obeyed without question and I declared it untrue when confronted by my mother—

whose father, a half-white, had lived for years as a recluse in the native style in Iao Valley—that the old man of Kawela was teaching me pagan ways.

In horror one day I heard the old man say "hemo ia oe kou lole—take off your clothes," which consisted of a pair of chopped-off dungarees.

"Hemo ia oe kou lole e holo oe a i'a i ka lua wai—take off your clothes and swim like a fish across the pool." My body froze and goose bumps formed everywhere on my skin.

"Awiwi—hurry."

I stood in sullen defiance, thinking: He is an old man, a servant. He cannot order me to do anything, anything.

"Au, keiki, Au! Swim, child, swim! Do not be afraid. They are with us."

I remained motionless.

"Auwe, heaha keia keiki kane? He kaika mahine puiwa paha?—What is this child, a frightened girl?"

Thoughts came to me of past fishing expeditions when I clung to the old man's back and he dove with me into holes filled with lobsters and certain crabs. He would choose as time allowed, pluck them from the coral walls, hand me two. Then, I could cling to him with only the use of my legs. In time I learned to rise to the surface alone, clinging with all my might to the two lobsters the old man had handed me. What excitement the first of these expeditions created! I leaped and danced around the crawling catch. We went down for a second take. Again two were brought up. On the reef above they were crushed, one then left as an offering on the kuula walls, the other fed to the akua in the pool. I was four or five then and wild with joy.

There were other days when he took me to great caverns swarming with fish of such brilliant colors you were nearly blinded by the reds, yellows, greens, blues and stripes. Above on the reef he would name them for me. Patiently he named them, these reef fish, aglow in cavern waters: the lau'ipala; the manini; the uhu; the ala'ihi; the kihikihi with its black, yellow and white stripes; the humuhumu with its blue patch on throat and vibrant yellow and red fins.

On one very special day, a sacred day in his life and mine as well—for I was linked to the family gods, the aumakua—he took me, clinging to his back, to the great sandy places under the sharp lava edges of Oahu's North Shore, to the places where the great sharks lazed in the light of day. Breaks in the lava walls sent shafts of light to sandy ocean floors and there we could see the sometimes-dreaded monsters rolling from side to side in harmless, peaceful rest. Shooting up to the surface, the old man would breathlessly tell me the names of this or that shark—names given them by his contemporaries.

"Why names?" I would ask wonderingly.

"Are they not our parents, our guardians—our aumakua? Did you not see the old chief covered with limu and barnacles? He is the chief, the heir of Kamohoalii. I used to feed him myself and clean the opala from his eyes. Now a younger member of my clan does that."

I could not absorb these calm, reassuring concerns of denizens I had been taught to dread from early years.

But had I not been down in their resting place, close enough to see yellow eyes, to almost feel the roughness of their skin scraping like sandpaper across my arms?

My dreams were wild for several nights and my parents, worried, held several conferences with the old man. He was chastened, but at my insistence we went several times more to the holes under coral ledges to see the aumakua lazing in the daytime hours.

And now, frozen at the edge of the green pool, I looked hatefully at this magnificent relic of a Hawaii that was long vanished. I loved him. There was no question I loved him deeply. Ours was a special kind of love of a man for a child.

I was blond-haired. Exposed for weeks to the summer sun when we made long stays at Kawela, I became almost platinum blond.

The old man was bearded, tall and thin. Still muscular. He was pure Hawaiian. Blond though my hair might be and my skin fair, I was nonetheless three-eighths Hawaiian. I think this captured the old man's fancy—often he would say to me in pidgin, "You one haole boy, yet you one Hawaiian. I know you Hawaiian—you mama hapa-haole, you papa hapa-haole. How come you so white? You hair ke'oke'o?" He would laugh, draw me close to him and rub his scruffy beard against my face as though in doing this he would rub some of his brownness off and ink forever the dark rich tones of a calabash into my pale skin.

It was love that finally led me to loosen the buttons of my shorts and kick them off and race plunging into the green pool. I swam with all the speed I could and reached in what seemed a very long time the opposite side. When I turned around, the old man was bent over with laughter. I had never seen him laugh with such gustatory abandon.

"Look you mea lii-lii. All dry up. Like one laho poka'o ka'o—like an old man's balls and penis. No can see now." He pointed and made fun of my privates, shrivelled from a combination of cold water and fear. I turned away from him and raced home, naked.

Four days later I walked past the pool, across the sharp lava flats to the old man's hut. Flies buzzed in legion. The stench was unbearable. I opened the door. Lying face up and straight across his little bed, the old man lay in the first stages of putrefaction. Sometime during my absence the old man had died. At midday? In the cool of night? In the late afternoon, the time of lengthening shadows and the gathering of the brilliant array of gold-orange and red off the coast of Kaena to the south facing the sea of Kanaloa? When did the old man die? Why did he die? Tears began to stream down my cheeks.

I shut the door of the shack and went to sit in the shade of the hau branches near the kuula—my heart was pounding so I could hardly breathe. What should I do? Tears rolled in little salty rivulets down my cheeks. I enjoyed the taste when the moisture entered my mouth at the corners of my lips.

What should I do? Some instinct compelled me not to go home and tell my family of the death of the old man and the putrefaction that filled the cottage. Perhaps I was too stunned—perhaps it was perversity.

The family was gathering for a large weekend revel. Aunts, uncles, cousins—all the generations coming together. Usually I enjoyed these congregations of the family. There would be masses of food, music, games and the great lauhala mats spread on the lawn near the sandy beach. Someone would make a bonfire and the talk would begin. I would sit at the edges of the inner circle of elders as they ruminated on past events. Old chiefs, kings, queens, great house parties—scandals and gossip of one sort or another would billow up from the central core of adults and leap into the air like flames. I absorbed the heat of this talk and greedily absorbed my heritage for they spoke of family members and their circles of friends, mostly people from royalist families, the Hawaiian and part-Hawaiian aristocracy during the last days of the Monarchy. I heard of this carriage or that barouche or landau, this house or that garden, this beautiful woman in love with so-and-so, or that abiding "good and patient" soul whose handsome husband dashed about town in a splendid uniform, lavishing on his paramour a beautiful house, a carriage and team, and flowing silk holokus fitted finely to her ample figure. O, the tales that steamed up from those gatherings on lauhala mats at Kawela's shores!

One of my great-aunts, an aberration of sorts, came once in a while for the weekend. She brought a paid companion and her Hawaiian maid. She looked like Ethel Barrymore and talked with an English accent. Her gossip was spicy, often vicious, and I loved it. She fascinated me as caged baboons fascinate some people who go to zoos.

She was also forbidding. I thought she had strange powers.

Often the old man had joined us during these family gatherings, and I would sit on his lap until I fell asleep.

There was something of great warmth and unforgettable charm in these gatherings. Even as the talk raged over romances, land dealings and money transactions long passed, I revelled in hearing about them and loved everyone there, particularly those who talked. There was an immense feeling of comfort and safety, of lovingness for me on those long nights of talk.

But now under the hau branches I scorned my family. I hated them. I held them responsible, for some unknown reason—a child's special reason I suppose; inexplicable and slightly irrational.

I decided not to tell them of the old man's death but to run down the path along the beach to the house where his relatives lived. I would tell them. They must rescue him from his rotting state; they must take him from the tomb of his stench-filled shack. I ran down along the beach, sometimes taking the path pressed into winding shape from human use in the middle of grass and pohuehue vines.

The men were at home, mending fishing nets. This was a good sign. I ran to the rickety steps leading upward to the porch where they sat working at their nets.

"The old man is dead," I said forcefully.

One of the young men looked down at me.

"Ma'ke."

"Yes, he's ma'ke. His body is stink. He ma'ke long time." They put down their mending tools and came in a body to the top of the stairs.

"How you know?" one of them asked.

"We just came back from Punalu'u. I went to the old man's house. I saw plenny flies. I open the door and see him covered with flies. It was steenk." I spoke partly in pidgin to give greater credibility to my message.

They fussed around, called into the house, held a brief conference and faced me again.

"You wen' tell anybody?"

"No, nobody."

The four men took the path at a run. I was under the hau bushes, catching my breath, when they flew past me heading back to their house. I sat for what seemed like hours in the shade of hau. My sister appeared at the side of the pool. I ran to fend her off. She caught the stench from the shack.

"Somthing stinks."

"The old man has fish drying outside his shack."

"Where is he?"
"Down on the reef fishing."
"When are you coming home?"
"Pretty soon."
"Mamma is looking for you—Uncle Willson is here with those brats," she referred to his adopted grandchildren. Uncle Willson was a grand old relic. Something quite unreal. He was brimming always with stories of the past.
"Aunt Emily has arrived with Miss Rhodes and that other one," my sister added, referring to the maid whom she hated.
The cottages would be bulging and perhaps tents would be set up for the servants.
My sister swung around abruptly and took the path back to our cottage. She was always purposeful in her movements.
"Tell Mamma I'll be home soon and kiss Uncle Willson and Aunt Emily for me."
"Don't stay too long. You'll get sunburned."
I walked past the pool. It seemed purer in its color today. Deep blue, deep green. I was crying again. The stench filled the air with a stronger, punishing aroma as the sun rose high and began the afternoon descent beyond Kaena Point. I walked along the reef; the tide was rising. I peeked into holes the old man had shown me, watched idly the masses of fish swimming in joyous aimlessness it seemed.
What ruled their lives? There was life and death among them. They were continually in danger of being devoured by larger fish. Some grew old and died, I suppose, they die of old age.
Death. Such an angry, total thing. There was no escaping it.
I looked back at the shack and shook my fists. The old man's nephews had returned with gleaming cans. They poured the liquid which filled them all around the little house. I rushed backed to the hau bushes as two of them threw lighted torches of newspaper at different places around the shack. Soon it was in flames which leaped to the sky; as the dry wood caught fire, it crackled angrily. The flies buzzed at a distance from the blaze as though waiting for it to die down. The heat was intense. The smell of burning rotting flesh unbearable.
I ran from the hau bushes toward the pool. One of the men saw me and yelled, "Go home, boy. Go home."
"Git da hell outa heah, you goddam haole," another one shouted. I was angry and stunned in not being accepted as a Hawaiian by the old man's nephews.
I ran around the pool at the side we seldom crossed. My family was

massing nearby to watch the fiery spectacle.

"What's happening, son?" my father asked with more than usual kindness.

I ran to my mother and hugged her thighs.

"The old man is dead. I found him. He was stinking. I ran down to tell his family."

"And now the bastards are burning him up," my father said. "It's against the law."

Aunt Emily had arrived on the arms of her companion and maid. Her handsome face pointed its powerful features to the center of the burning mass.

"What is happening?" she asked in Hawaiian.

"Our caretaker died. Been dead for several days. The boy found him."

"What are they doing?"

"It's illegal. They're cremating him without going through the usual procedures."

Aunt Emily blasted forth with a number of her original and unrepeatable castigations. Everyone listened. They were gems of Hawaiian metaphor.

Uncle Willson and his man servant arrived.

"The poor old bastard finally died. He was the best fisherman of these parts in his younger days. No one could beat him. As a boy he was chosen to go down to the caverns and select the shark to be taken to use for the making of drums. His family were fishermen. One branch was famed as kahunas. He was a marvel in his day."

"But Willy," Aunt Emily was saying in a commanding tone. "Those brutes are burning his body. The boy here says it was rotten. He'd been dead for several days. The whole thing's a matter for the Board of Health authorities. The police should be called."

"No, no!" I screamed.

"Emily dear," Great Uncle Willson intervened. "He is one of us. His ohana, those young men, are a part of us. Leave them alone. They are doing what they think best."

I had gone from my mother to my nurse Kulia, a round, happy sweet-smelling Hawaiian woman.

"No cry, baby. No cry. We all gotta die sometime. Da ole man was real old."

"Not that old," I whimpered.

Aunt Emily cast one of her iciest looks at me.

"Stop that snivelling. Stop it this instant. What utter foolishness to cry that way over a dirty, bearded old drunk."

She turned to my mother,

"This child was allowed to be too much with that old brute. I think his attachment was quite unnatural—quite unnatural."

"Another one of your theories, Aunt Emily," my mother snapped.

"Not a thing but good common sense. Look at him clinging to Kulia and whimpering like a girl."

Kulia took me away. We walked on the beach.

How I hated Aunt Emily's Ethel Barrymore profile and her English accent.

Late that day, in the early evening, the old man's nephews came back and carried off his charred remains in the empty cans of kerosene. No one ever found out what they did with them.

When did the old man die? Why did he die? This I will never know. We called him Bobada, but I remember from something Great Uncle Willson said on the night the shack was burned that Bobada's real name was Pali Kapihe.

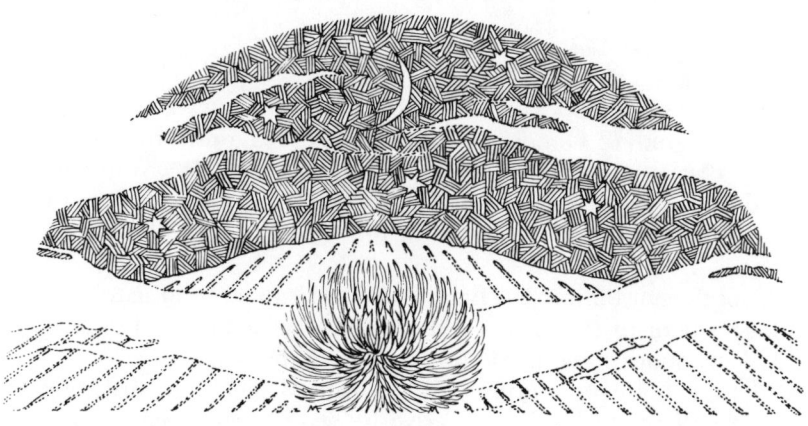

Today Ees Sad-dy Night

There is really no good reason for celebrating in our memories the importance of one day over another, yet certain recollections glow with a particular iridescent beauty and have the power to fix a particular day firmly within the body of our remembrance. Shadows, or a fragrance, the color of something, a sound, the look of the skies, of clouds, recall things to us about certain people and away we go, carried on the magic carpet of our thoughts to the past—distant or near.

As the years add Saturday afternoons to my recollections of weekends, most of them are forgotten ones. But one I remember explicitly. It stubbornly haunts my memory of a visit I paid to the island of Maui when I was sixteen; and it might have been the time when our friend Arabella de Frecency was swept into the dark valley of madness, from which she was never to return.

In remembering this particular Saturday, the large form of Haleakala Mountain looms to become the first chiaroscuro fragment of my recollection.

From Paia—flat and at the seashore—the extinct volcano rises to its peak slightly above ten thousand feet. It dominates Maui. It is the island's outstanding geological attribute. From Paia the land sweeps upward in a magnificent rise—green and verdant in the foothills—to Makawao. Beyond that it appears as a mauve, yellow, and deep purple mosaic interspersed with accents of red or pink; or, formed in black, the clusters of coniferous evergreens are planted to surround and protect (from the lusty winds of the slopes) scattered empires: some large, most of them the small summer homes or "mountain houses" of Maui's residents.

On one of these empires Arabella de Frecency lived alone with two maidservants in a large rambling, and weather-beaten ranch house built many years before by her father. Above Makawao, on the way to Kula and south of Olinda, a small, rock-infested, dusty road led to the house that was protected from view of the outside world and the winds by a high wall of eucalyptus trees, and by a thicker one—though not of the great height of the "gum" trees—of a variety of cedar.

Cool thin air bit into the nostrils at this altitude, air infused with the pungent odor of eucalyptus and the cedars which seemed to thrive at this level about three thousand feet above the sea.

"Faster, Okihara, a little faster!" Uncle Malcolm had urged on his tiny chauffeur. Plantation man that he was, he respected leisure time and had learned over the years to make the best possible use of "time off." The schedule of work on the great sugar plantations of Hawaii being still a regimen of twelve hours each day for bosses and workmen alike, leisure was pursued with inordinate intensity, compressed in the hours between two o'clock on Saturday afternoon to a related hour of the next day—the Sunday following it. Uncle Malc hated the loss of a single moment when he undertook the long, winding drive to Makawao to visit Arabella de Frecency.

"Ees good, ees good, spasiba!" Mary Kharkov shouted. "Ouch! Go queek stop! Queek! One more dreenk can take! Yahoooo! Meester Malc, smart man, Meester Malc!"

"Control your tongue, old vooman!" Peter Kharkov said, and continued, "You must be getting drunk! Perhaps the altitude is too much for you in your old age!"

"Whoooopeeee, Meester Malc! Gooood riding, huh? And you, Peter, I'm not old age! Today I'm young cheeken! Today ees Sad-dy night!"

"Hush, old vooman! Now ees day! Tonight ees night! Maybe you getting drunk already!"

"Never mind, Peter! Mary is just letting off a little steam."

"She vill steam morning time! Big head, big, big head!"

"Ha! Ha! Good air breathink! Vat da hell vee vorry for da big head!"

The old Packard touring limousine swerved as Okihara, still being urged on by Uncle Malcolm, sped the car around a sharp turn.

"A-yeeee!" Mary exploded. "Whoooopeeee, go like hell, old girl, go!"

Uncle Malcolm chuckled. He chuckled only. He was never given to the loud guffaw. A huge man, his appearance combined the rawboned virility of a Victor McLaglen and the ascetic grace of a William Butler Yeats. "You will like Arabella," he said to me. "She's a real paniolo—a cowpuncher of the first order!" and he chuckled again. "Now isn't that a God-damned name for a real cowpuncher? Arabella!" He hung on the sound of the word.

"I like Mees Arabella! Good time plenty time me an' Mees Arabella before old times! No more da viskey! Vee drinking okolehao! Yipeeee, Mees Arabella! Na Zdarodni!"

"In Ukrania I trow you to da volves, old vooman. You are a disgrace to the saints, praise our dear Lord!"

"You only good for making saddle, Petoi. You making too many saddle. Forget how to make da whoopee! Meester Malc, you tell Peter shutup and have good time!"

Okihara managed the large automobile with perseverance, but clumsily. In spite of bumps and swerves and the strange chokings of the engine as he shifted gears to meet the challenge of steeper grades, he brought us ever closer to Arabella de Frecency by manipulation—persistent and dedicated—of the aging limousine.

"Okihara manages this old museum piece quite expertly."

Uncle Malc's remark was a rationalization for it was a great convenience for us to have a driver this afternoon. There would be heavy drinking (practiced almost ceremoniously by my elderly friends) and I was under the legal age to operate a vehicle on the public highway. To have someone to drive us home was a fortunate luxury. Okihara was usually let off on Saturday afternoons to pursue his own diversions. So even in the privacy of his thoughts Uncle Malcolm did not wish to discredit Okihara's handling of the car.

Below us, the narrow central plain, dividing west Maui from the huge bulk of Haleakala, stretched from one coast line to the other. It was thrilling to see the expanse of this section of the island down below made so intimate—so easily possessed by height and distance.

"Arabella's father was my great friend! A fine rancher! A superb horseman! A very fine man!"

Mary Kharkov had slipped into a quiet, dozing state, spent of the raucous hilarity, the *joie de vivre,* and its concomitant explosions which she had shown during the earlier moments of the drive from Paia.

"Many saddle an' bridle I make Meester Tonio."

"He was a good customer, Peter. He appreciated your talent."

"Him good friend, too. Mary an' me come from Rhoosia over forty year before. Meester Tonio, he come plantation stable. He make friend. I think old boss tell heem I good for make da saddle. He speak one, two word Rhoosian. Is like music! Only one, two word, but is like music!"

Anthony de Frecency, an old-world aristocrat, having drifted to Hawaii in his early manhood, had become one of the great ranching personalities in the *fin-de-siecle* era of cattle raising in Hawaii. I'd heard many things about this interesting man from both my father and Uncle Malc. They had told me about how well he got along with his Hawaiian cowboys, and how perfectly he spoke the Hawaiian language. He was famed for the loyalty he had won from the cowboys and for the adoration he had won from his four daughters. I also knew that after his death the ranch had been abandoned by all his children, except Arabella.

"I no talk English—one, two word, maybe—but I look Mister Tonio. His eyes talk. I know inside good man. One, two word Rhoosian. But is enough! Outside him like old country boyar. You know what is boyar, Mister Malc?" and as Uncle Malc had indicated with a shaking of his head that he didn't know what boyar meant, Peter had continued, "In old country, boyar is high man, big shot—landowner before come Lenin—before come dis son-of-a-bitch bolsheviki revolutzie!"

"Mr. Tonio's people were Hungarian. Hungary is near your old country."

"Yah, but now, Mister Malc, me an' Mary ... look this old vooman, to sleep! ... ve American! Even come Hawaii, ve American!"

Okihara had brought us safely to the turnoff—the rocky, narrow cow trail which meandered for several miles before it led through the gates of the de Frecency ranch house. We lurched into the narrow road. Arabella had had the gates opened for us.

"Be a good sport, my boy, and close the gate."

I left the car quickly and started for the gate. Okihara had begun to arrange things in a complicated maneuvering of gears, brakes, and the ignition switch, to allow him to leave the car safely stanced while he performed the irksome necessity of closing gates: one of the standing irritations to be contended with in cattle country.

"Never mind, Okihara, our boy will shut the gate."

"O, too much tank you!"

When I returned and we were once again sketchily in motion, Uncle Malc said, "Didn't dare let Okihara leave the car for fear he'd never be able to start it up again and get us to Arabella's. Be a hell of a note if we had to walk the last few miles!"

"Valk? Valk?" old Mary shouted. "I valk for see Mees Arabella, any time!" The stop had awakened her.

"Shut up, you old brood mare! Go back to sleep. We enjoyed peace for a few moments," Peter Kharkov snapped in Russian.

"Ha! I no sleep now! 'Nough sleep. Pretty soon ve see Mees Arabella! We have big drink! Whooopeee!" and then, launching into Russian, she said only for Peter's benefit, "I wonder what elegant names I can think up for you in a hurry!"

I had quickly asked for translations, unconcerned over the possibility of being considered "nosey." In my upbringing, which was partly Hawaiian, being nosey was equal to some strange state of defilement—to being, in effect, leprous.

The old Packard took the rustic driveway with admirable determination and grace.

"You sure, Mister Malc, Miss Arabella no care when you bringing me an' Mary her house this afternoon?"

"Nonsense, Peter! She will enjoy having you!"

On some Saturday afternoons, Uncle Malcolm would stop at Peter and Mary's house in the plantation village. This had become somewhat of a ritual after the death of his wife, Katherine. Peter and Mary were excellent drinking partners; but beyond this, at a less superficial level, there was rapprochement. Barriers of culture and language were strangely dissolved by this closeness of the spirit which passed between my uncle and the old Russian couple; and it would become clearly apparent to me why he had insisted on them joining us in the visit to Arabella de Frecency. It was a matter of the kindred—the basic underlying force of loneliness and individualism—that could hold these four beings together comfortably, if only for a few hours, to pursue gaiety and pleasure as they saw fit.

In trying to speak of the sense and nonsense of this fragment of my past, it occurs to me that only Arabella achieved the total escape into sanctified oblivion. This I know for a fact. It was true that Uncle Malcolm moved far in this direction as he completed his lonely span of widowhood; but he did not totally escape reality until his dying day. Mary and Peter's separation was an ineluctable one, forced upon them by the act of emigration and the myriad circumstances that this unleashed.

Arabella was accustomed to solitude; and for a time she had thrived in her life on the mountain slope with her two maids—one an older, the other a younger Japanese woman—and her menagerie of pet goats, sheep, turkeys, chickens, peacocks, cows, and horses (some of these of historic importance in the de Frecency saga). But today Arabella had eagerly awaited our arrival. Saturday afternoon, alone on the slope of Haleakala, can be a lesson in abject solitude. If you are inclined, it is a perfect setting for ascetic detachment. If you are not, it can be a hell of smoldering solitude and loneliness. She had fortified herself with large straight drinks of okolehao in anticipation of our coming. In her most intact pair of lole ahina (blue jeans), her hair somewhat combed under the sombrero style lauhala hat, she greeted us with lusty gusts of expressions that would have made her late, well-born, and sedulously decorous English mother bristle with annoyance.

The meeting between Arabella and Mary was epic: a kind of explosive phenomenon similar in a certain way to a volcanic eruption —one of milder vehemence. They wept heartily, and embraced with a vigor that startled even Uncle Malcolm who was not easily startled. And why? For no reason that was basic, sensible, or, if you like, rational, Miss de Frecency and old Mary came together like long separated members of an esoteric and precious sisterhood. It was Saturday afternoon, and the "girls," as Uncle Malc was to designate them later in the day, were unconsciously jubilant over the release from the cares of ranch and plantation life, and the promise of riotous fun for the next thirty or so hours.

"Ve come with Mister Malc, Miss Arabella, you not minding?"

"Hell no, Mary! This is wonderful!" Then glancing in my direction, "And over here's the young sport!" Her steel blue eyes sparkled with mischief. "Come over here, son, and let me see you. Ah, a bit fat—like your father, n'est-ce-pas?" She grasped my hand in a formidably familiar way. "How do you do, young man?" Her hands were rough, her grip hard; but something in the clasp indicated friendliness and warmth.

"And Peter! You old Cossack, you!"

"Not Cossack! I'm making saddle for horse. Many saddle I'm making for your daddy, Mister Tonio. Not Cossack!"

Arabella had gone into a version of the hopak, Mary encouraging the performance with a wild clapping of her hands and a raucous atonal version of music that she deemed appropriate accompaniment to Arabella's flight into the mawkish.

So this was Arabella de Frecency: famous as a horsewoman; held by most people to be a bit more than eccentric; the sister of a nationally famous violinist; and of a brother, also well known, who pursued the career of artist in a Parisian attic—or was it a gutter?—as some of the old folks would ask. So this was a daughter of old Tony de Frecency: the only woman in the Territory of Hawaii who had made it her business to break horses! She had even trained polo ponies for the rich Maui Calhouns. Her skill in this occupation was celebrated in the ranching set. She bridled horses with a touch that was like fine music or poetry. Elegant and famous people had come and gone in Arabella's lifetime, paying brief and exciting visits to the ranch, some of them carrying tales of her superb horsemanship to the far corners of the earth. All of this I knew from hearsay!

In spite of the hoydenish outburst of greeting, the coarse hands, the cowboy clothes, and the outlandish hat, there was manner and form in Arabella. Even as she rolled Durham tobacco cigarettes, she kept a finesse of movement. Her voice was excellently pitched, the words said with a fine regard for enunciation as though she had never abandoned elocution instructions as rendered her and her sisters by an elderly English governess who had directed their lives for so many years.

"Okihara will bring in some supplies. We came fortified."

"That was not necessary, Malc."

"I bring boil cheeken and cucumba!"

"Glorious, Mary! A perfect pupu (tidbit) with oke!" And then she directed her words to my uncle again. "But you should not have brought anything, Malc. After all, this is a ranch house—and quite a self-sufficient one, I might add!"

I lingered outside. Something in the atmosphere of the place held me: the old house, weathering perfectly, its shingled exterior greying and mossy in the shaded areas, the broad coniferous hedge that bordered the drive from the entrance gate, the great koa trees spreading over the lawns, and the sharp perfume of eucalyptus hanging in the air invisible and potent, adding its touch to the dreamlike quality of the moment. In the large entrance court, caught within two jutting wings of the house, several species of flowers were now profusely in bloom. They seemed incongruously petite, almost ridiculous if you stopped to think of them as actually growing in the tropics. Like Arabella's English mother, they belonged to another atmosphere where air and sunlight and seasonal upheavals combined to produce the environmental balance that give such flowers their character. More than this, they were out of rhythm with the affinities which gave Arabella her uniqueness—that made her, a woman and a haole, still able to be a paniola. Because of the unseemly character of the colorful annuals, the garden assumed a chimerical quality. It was unseemly and out of place, almost a ghostly setting. I could not attach it to the broader world of growing things that established the reality of Hawaii. It was an unique hybrid atmosphere—as individual and unpredictable as the de Frecencys were in their behavior.

Laughter flowed out from the French doors, and I could hear old Mary's rasping voice painfully forming a continuous torrent of words that came from a free floating euphoria: the results of the drinks, the thin cool air, and the Rabelaisian heart she had brought with her from

Russia forty years ago. I thought of famous horses, of great parties, of the small army of inhabitants that had lived here in the hey-day of the ranch. Laughter had flowed from the same doors then, and the de Frecency life had become a legend. People remembered their visits here in the past with a sense of profound gratitude as though they were in possession of a fine object—fragile and irreplaceable.

Several peacocks had gathered in the driveway near the entrance court. Noticing me, a stranger, they approached cautiously. There were several white birds in the flock; and I was struck by how ordinary they looked—like white turkeys really—alongside their gorgeous blue-green companions. Already two brilliantly colored cocks had erected their gaudy tail feathers to shape the great fan for which this haughty fowl is so noted. The younger of the maids came out from the back of one of the wings of the house and immediately the exotic birds dashed in a chorus toward her. It was feeding time. Peacocks had been a stubbornly romantic feature of my father's recollections of life on his father's ranch at Mikilua on the island of Oahu. It was easy to see that here the peacocks were a living fragment of the de Frecency dream.

"Do you like my birds?" Arabella had approached from behind me.

"They're beautiful. Their feathers are in excellent condition. You don't see them look this fine in the Zoo at home in Honolulu."

"I'll say you don't. I feed my birds excellently and let them run free. And then, too, I think the coolness up here has something to do with keeping their feathers healthy. Why don't you come in? I've come out to ask you in."

"I'm enchanted by your place. It has a dreamlike quality. I wanted to stay out here for a while and enjoy it."

"A young romantic—like my sister, Ina! She's the famous musician."

"Yes, I know!"

"Ina used to dream away long hours about the place. A dreamer that was as good on a horse as any of us. She had a tree house in that eucalyptus." She pointed to one of the mammoth trees. "She used to climb up there and read—and practice on the fiddle, sometimes. But what awful scratchings when she first began! She was a very good horsewoman. Really an excellent rider. She took Dad's famous Arab Napoleon, once, and rode sixteen miles to fetch old Doctor Hoskins. Mother was sick. She was English. Shamelessly so! Even fifty years of living in Hawaii couldn't reduce her Englishness! I think she was very unhappy here. So did Dad, I think. 'My good and devoted Rose,' he would say, 'How she fretted about things. She could never shed her little county habits.' One of the families 'of the county,' the Merediths! She was Rose Meredith. There was a duke and an earl somewhere in the family tree."

Her eyes were misty; her voice, now soft and monotonous in its intonation, forming word groups streaming out compulsively. "Strange marriage—strange that two people such as they were could meet here nearly sixty years ago and marry! My father's family was Hungarian. They had lived in France for a generation or so, which accounts for the *de* Frecency. Otherwise it would have been *von!* He came to Hawaii on a frigate as the guest of one of his French cousins who commanded the ship. He liked the look of things here and stayed. King Lunalilo was on the throne. Mother was born here. Her father was one of the early British consuls to Hawaii. She was schooled in England, poor soul!"

Okihara brought our offerings from the car—he had parked it far down where it would not obstruct passage in the drive. Arabella politely told him where to find the maids and then continued her autobiographical chatter. I was delighted that she was so talkative. One way of knowing about the old days was to hear people talk about them.

"Father was the last of the romantic individualists—a pipi laho hihiu! Do you understand Hawaiian? I speak a perfect cowboy patois."

"You said your father was like a renegade bull!"

"Now, that's wonderful—a renegade bull! I actually said, 'wild bull,' but stop to think of it, all wild bulls are renegade, and they are all ruggedly individualist! Dad was a pipi laho hihiu, an old renegade bull. Mother was all lace and roses and spicy cakes! I was a tiny little thing when she died. Father raised us, God bless him! I was the youngest." She stopped and looked beyond the cedar-lined drive to the towering eucalyptus trees and beyond. "Look up there! Old Haleakala! The patriarch of our island! To ride a horse up that long winding slope . . . taking you up slowly, always a little closer . . . stopping to look back down over the little neck that lets the sea come close on either side! I love it when they swelter in the dust down there on those damned plowed-up sugar fields! I love it when it's new and fresh and green with the cane growing. It's so earth and sea, all at one time. But I love it more up above! Even the horses would snort at the earthy scene below. Above, old Haleakala! . . . the coldness of the moon . . . the very moon itself . . . the moon gave us a piece of itself! And where else in the world can you find the silver sword growing? Perhaps on the moon . . . no place on earth that I know! Haleakala . . . 'the House of the Sun!' Only for the daytime hours . . . at night she's the moon! I have stood at the crater's edge in the moonlight . . . I have stood in the moon! It's magic, sheer magic! It is sheer glory! One is at one with the moon . . . the summit is the moon at night! The House of the Sun is the moon! . . . It should be approached with reverence! . . . on a fine horse! . . . as all of mine were!" Then, without warning, rage overcame her and she shouted, "That God-damned road has ruined me! Absolutely ruined me! Has your uncle said anything to you about that God-damned new road?" She turned away; and silence, dark as the night itself, came between us. Then, almost contritely, in a voice that held a sob, she said, "I used to take riding parties to the summit on my precious horses. It was also my living! Now everyone motors! . . . they simply race to the summit now!" She made a mad gesture with her arms as though she were driving a car at a wild speed. "They say it twists and turns viciously, and it's as narrow as a hair! I don't know! I don't know . . . I've never been on it! . . . *and I never will!*"

The words poured out in a torrent of sound; the emphasis she gave certain ones briefly inhibited the flow as rest marks halt the continuation of a gush of notes in a musical score. I was too young to have these thoughts of anger and bitterness thrust upon me. They were bewildering and odd. I felt like screaming with laughter. It was so funny that this legendary, sophisticated woman should confide in me, a youth—a callow, unformed, ogling youth. I stood transfixed, wordless, as she continued the outpouring. What could I say? If a single word of sympathy formed, I would blurt it out and then laugh—a reflex, a nervous callow reflex—and this would be too much for my ego to bear. I wanted to create the impression that I was dramatically beyond my years in personal development.

"My horses! My precious babies! I had twenty-eight horses. Now I've got three . . . destroyed the rest. Destroyed them . . . all fine creatures! . . . every one broken to bit by myself and Kupili, my helper." Gesticulation, inflection, and facial expression were employed exquisitely to add to the luster of the tragedy. "God-damned road!" and with this Arabella clapped her hands vehemently, then let forth a hollow, empty laugh.

Now it would come! my callow response. I let a flow of dream-images come into my consciousness to dispel the impulse. I saw riders on mounts that were splendidly robust, with shiny coats and alert eyes, picking their way fleetly through the tufts of fern and grass and the twisted, lovely clumps of pukiawe, a gnarled bush growing only on the higher reaches of Haleakala, as though they were being drawn to the crater's summit by a supernatural attraction.

"Arabella!" Uncle Malcolm called from the door.

The gods were with me! Uncle Malc's hoarse and masculine voice crashed into the moment like a great felled tree trunk splashing into the still waters of a lagoon.

"God-damned name! I've always hated it! Mother gave it to me in honor of a damned favorite maiden aunt! Coming!" She turned to me, "Be a good fellow and take Okihara to the little butcher down on the highway. I keep a slaughtered beef there. Old Chan Wah, the butcher, has cut some steaks for us. Go down and fetch them. I'm afraid if we send Okihara alone we mightn't get the steaks until morning."

I was more than willing. Arabella de Frecency had won my heart. She was pure poetry—lyric poetry—to me!

"Be back in a jiffy!"

"Do so! I'll have Taruko start up the charcoal."

"The boy here plays the piano, Arabella. He plays very well!" Uncle Malcolm announced shortly after dinner when we had gathered in the living room.

"And we've been for hours without music! How cruel!" Arabella rushed to an old square rosewood instrument and opened it. "I take excellent care of this piano! Have it tuned every year. It was Mother's. Carl Burkmeister comes up every June to tune it. It came round the Horn centuries ago. Everybody's old pianos came round the Horn centuries ago!"

"Play for me Cheechonia!" Old Mary rose tipsily from her chair and twirled about the room, wheezing out the platitudinous song.

"Not yet, Mary, that comes later. After a while. Play! Play anything! Wait!" and, cogitating deeply, Arabella sought through memory until: "Play Love Nest! Da di ta ta, tum ti ta ta di dum dum, little love nest, way out in the west!"

I had never heard this popular ditty; and, no matter how hard I tried to dig into memory on the off-chance it may have been stored there in a neglected or forgotten corner, and, with this effort at recollection, come leaping out of its hiding place, I could not play a single note to fulfill Arabella's request.

"Don't you know it? It was a very popular song some years ago!"

The impulse to laugh recurred. This was utter tyranny! Aside from its patent rudeness, I hated the impulse because it was so hard to suppress it.

"Da ti tim ti, ta ta ti tum tum . . ."

"Yipeeee!"

"That's it! That's it! You're getting it! By golly, young man, you're terrific! Tum ti da da, the little love nest, just built for two! By golly, we'll have all the music we want tonight. You're just marvelous, pet, just marvelous!"

I stopped for a moment when I suspected that her interest in "Love Nest" had atrophied, as do so many enthusiastic outbursts brought on by drinking.

"Keep going, boy, keep going! Da da ti da . . . Malc, you old li'o laho, go see to our drinks!" I was surprised to see that Arabella's interest in "Love Nest" had not ended after all.

Uncle Malcolm and old Peter had sat with their drinks in their chairs across the room, watching the genesis of our vaudevillian effort. Even Peter seemed amused. Perhaps there was, after all, something quite funny in this. My impulse then was not too aberrant.

"O, such dancing that went on here when I was a chit! The sky was the limit! The Charleston, the Bunny Hug, the Black-Bottom! We danced them all!"

Old Mary twirled and sang, her voice hoarse now with the heroic effort she spent trying to follow Arabella's rendition. Peter muttered phrases under his breath, aimed undoubtedly at the high-spirited Mary. Uncle Malcolm went to the dining room to get more drinks.

"Have one with us, young fellow! Just one!" he offered me.

I continued faking the melody of the trite little song which had so captivated Arabella. Then, automatically it seemed, I began to play an old Hawaiian tune, "Ua Like No A Like." Its music was in character with Arabella's beautiful living room. Nobly proportioned and furnished in an eclectic style, veering toward Empire, it held many lovely pieces of furniture and objets d'art. Two large mirrors reflected these contents and the fine grain in the native woods of the wall and floor. An Aubusson rug, spread over the entire center portion of the floor, was patterned in large salmon-pink roses. This softly lighted room belonged to another time, another epoch, a time more generous of amenities and dreams. As I dawdled at the piano, trying to keep Arabella happy and at ease with my playing, I was able to make a very careful study of the large old room.

"This is just the way dear Mother had it," Arabella said abruptly as though she could read my mind, and then she popped up and headed toward the kitchen. I played "Love Nest" again and waited. When she did not return soon, I left the piano and hurried out-of-doors before old Mary could notice my retreat and raise a ruckus over it. I wished to capture one more feasting view of the darkened surrounding world. I had been ambling slowly around the area of the terrace and the drive for sometime when I noticed that Arabella was again at my side—as she had been so many hours past, earlier in the evening.

"Isn't it beautiful, . . . too maddeningly so . . . too delicious! 'Oceans of time, whose waters of deep woe are brackish with the salt of human tears!'" Arabella dramatically quoted from Shelley. "God-damned words of some faded rose of a word slinger countryman of my dearly beloved faded rose of a mamma! 'The flower that smiles today tomorrow dies.'" Then she was silent—ominously silent.

The impulse to laugh had left me and for the first time in my sixteen years of life I was burdened with the great weight of sadness that touches us far beneath the surface of ordinary feelings.

Arabella spoke again: "Look at that superb mountain! My hero and my nemesis. My moon! My lonely moon! My love and my undoing . . . my moon. No more horseback parties to the summit. I will never look again into the burnished pit, at the cinders and dust of the crater of my moon. My house of sun of daytime . . . moon of the night. Such sounds, such beautiful sounds, and such clouds . . . such clouds!" She began to sob, and her remaining utterances were intertwined like fragile vines on the framework of her sobs. "But how painful, how painful it all is at times!"

The urgent reality of her sobbing and her words were like a tortured, supplicating litany addressed to massive darkness and its abstract powers. With the force of a gushing stream, the experience—almost a sacred ritual in its inevitability—thrust me out of my state of giddy uncertainty of a few moments ago into a new realm of consciousness. In a moment of unexpected crisis, fierce in its intensity, I had shed another petal from the flower of my youth.

Night was falling swiftly. The voices within the house beckoned us to come. They were familiar—alive! But I am afraid that at this moment Arabella did not hear them. Other voices of a time past—of another timbre and tonality—of another world—beckoned her from the gorgeous dizzy heights of Haleakala Mountain.

"Shall we go in?" I asked timorously.

She offered her arm in the hesitating, langorous manner of the aged. I took it, and held it tight against my body.

Princess of the Night Rides

Riding at full gallop through the darkened streets offered a powerful sense of freedom—of utter release from the mundane, the common, the plodding. Scented air, cooling wind, and unrevealing darkness combined deliciously to fill her spirit with a moment's relief from a sustained and gnawing melancholy. A shadow of emptiness—of a massive ennui—had settled upon the princess's life. The regimen of training at the schools in England, befitting an heir to a throne; the august watchfulness and stately admonitions of Mr. Harrington Thorpe, her guardian abroad, offered little now to subdue an enormous restlessness—an increasing wildness of heart.

Time and again recently, she had taken her little mare, Damozel, on nocturnal galloping sprees through the night-lit, silent streets of Honolulu. The mare was a tangible link with England—a horse of Arabian strain, given her by an admirer. She had brought the splendid animal across the world's two great oceans and the whole stretch of North America—from east to west—to her home in the Islands of Hawaii. "What a beautiful horse! She will ride in our parades! What a spirited animal, as befitting the Princess Victoria Kaiulani as her garden at Waikiki!" some of her people had said. Now, one of her greatest pleasures was to ride into the night when it was cool. After spending seven long years in the wintry temperatures of Northern Europe, she found the languid tropical air of her island birthplace almost intolerable. It was a luxurious joy to ride in the sunless dark of the night.

Rumor of her nightly riding excursions had spread through the town. The sophisticated foreigner smiled and passed off the rides laconically as just another expression of aristocratic eccentricity. The native whites, who had recently seized the government from the princess's aunt, interpreted her behavior as another proof of monarchical decay. Caustically, they might say: "How unlady-like! It's something a common native would do—if they dared to go out at night! Is it any wonder we took the government out of their hands?" Her own people awoke with the sound of galloping hooves, and, knowing instantly the mount and its rider, they grieved. Theirs was the knowledge of kinship; and their concern was from the heart. They were of one thought: "She is troubled! Our princess grieves for Hawaii!" Their lament was: "Aloha ino o kau wahine alii pio, pua ui loa ka aina!"

Her father, an aging Scot, now given over to much brooding and silence, looked upon these nightly rides with an unyielding disapproval. They were at variance with the dream of perfection he had nurtured for his daughter from the moment of her birth. They were irascible, aberrant—befitting the hoyden or irresponsible half-witted empresses, but not the stately young woman, the Milo Venus in her beauty, whom he had sired and sent to his mighty England to be rigorously trained within "the royal set" for the role of leadership. Some "sensible" people agreed with her father. The incredible beauty of the princess, her intellect and refinement, combined, they said, to make the spectacle of her furious night rides a thing of strangeness.

But no one made light of these erratic nightly excursions—not even the foreigner with his knowing and sly appraisal—for in them there was an element of regal fatality. They contained a heavy and uncomfortable reality; they were unexpected and strange—perhaps even ghostly, like the schools of red fish that had swarmed into the quiet waters of Honolulu Harbor a few weeks before the last king of Hawaii, her mother's brother, "Uncle David," had died. The night rides exacted their toll of response from listening ears. Some grieved; some smarted with the prick of guilt; some made cynical allusion to "royal decadence" and the like. Everyone reacted.

Giving into the demands of a towering will, the princess galloped in the darkness and let the cooling winds of night bring passing comfort to her tormented body. "I find the heat more oppressive than the annexationists," she wrote her aunt, the ex-queen, who was in Washington. "My body is covered with rash, and I sometimes find it difficult to breathe. I ride at night, on occasion, to Nuuanu. The trade winds are lively there, and give me the only relief I've known from the oppressive heat. I guess I am no longer a native Hawaiian in this respect; my body is at odds with the warm air of the tropics."

In the subdued and balmy darkness of another island night, she was riding once more on the narrow road leading from Waikiki into the sleep-drenched town of Honolulu. Words and images tumbled in her thoughts, like waves breaking one upon the other at Kaalawai. She had brought the mare out of a hard gallop and subdued her, chafing, into a walk. The animal breathed hard. "Easy, Damozel, easy! We both needed that sprint!"

Memory of the tall Guards officer filled a corner of her mind. Had she loved him? She could not be certain. Had he loved her? An infatuation perhaps—nothing more. Their paths had been officially separated by edicts over which they had no control: one took him to India, and the other brought her home to the islands in the Pacific. The little mare had remained a bond with the Guards officer. It was his parting gift to her. The mare snorted and breathed in deep gasps to recapture her wind from the hard, fast spurt of a moment ago. "Easy, Damozel! Easy! It's this clammy air, this heat. You would run five times as far in England and not be gasping so to catch your breath!"

England! The cool, foggy air and its green downs, the forests and castles, the clever people of her acquaintance, were a fixed part of her now. "How can we forget England, eh, Damozel?" But Captain Beautemps? What about him? He is far away now—only a figment in a large assortment of memories.

The mare started at a falling branch, swept down by the winds of the night, "Easy, Damozel," she whispered solicitously. "Nothing to be afraid of! No one can see us now! No one!" The horse was calmed, but kept an attitude of alertness.

"Thank God for Koa," she murmured as though the mare was another person. She saw Koa standing on the lanai at Ainapua, strong, gentle, and abiding. He was a prince—he was Hawaiian. And he had spent a single frigid winter in England, pursuing, he had told her, the subject of political economy at the University of London. They had met only once in England. They had met often as children in Hawaii. She summoned the image of her father. Why is he so against Koa? Bearded, his body starting to bend now and his face assuming the gaunt lines of age, her father had grown formidable in his demonstrations of disapproval. In connection with Koa, it was expressed mostly by silence, and occasionally, by faintly suggested criticisms. Koa was not business-minded enough! He ought to be, as he was poor! Koa was not serious enough in matters of government! He ought to be, in order to fight the missionary opposition! These views were expressed during long sessions at table where talk had, at times, flared into loud outbursts.

The effect upon both father and daughter became, every day, more apparent. Scarcely a night passed without an argument. The talk in these exchanges had narrowed down to a single subject. Tonight it had been of particular vehemence. They had both exceeded the usual limits in the taking of wines. This had spurred on their words:

"What are you doing with your life? You are throwing it away!"

"Does it matter, Father? Does it really matter?"

"Indeed, it does! Why do you ride at night? It is quite mad! It is dangerous! There are whispers about it all over the town!"

"By whom, and why? Do you think I care? I have harmed no one in my rides at night! Not a soul!"

It would have been unthinkable in England to ride out this way at night. For one thing, it would be too cold most of the time. "I tried, Damozel. I tried very hard in England to make the best of my opportunity. It was not always easy, as you might know, you Arab of England!" She patted the horse's neck affectionately and was answered with a soft snort. "Perhaps I was away too long—too, too long! Those dreadful last three years! They were a vigil! We wandered aimlessly from one continental spa to another, my tiresome, hired companions and I. My father, bless his heart, joined me in the last year while we waited for the haole revolutionists here to sanction my return. Those were bitter days. . . . and now . . . ?" She cast her eyes to the heavens. "Can I forgive? Should I forgive? They say one cannot live without forgiving."

A few days before this, she had written her friend, the Marquise de Crecy, who lived near Combray in France: "Last week some Americans came to my house and knocked rather violently at the door, and when they had stated their cause, they wished to know if it would be permissable for the EX-princess to have her picture taken with them. Oh will they never leave us alone? They have taken everything away from us and it seems there is left but little, and that little our very life itself. We live now in such a semi-retired way that people wonder if we even exist anymore. I, too, wonder, and to what purpose?" She patted Damozel's arching, graceful Arabian neck again.

How sweet and cool the air was; how marvelous a sedative the night and its shadows. "Sweet creature—sweet, sweet creature!" She murmured out of love for her mount. "Father keeps the illusion that I am still the languid, big-eyed child of fourteen who left here nine years ago. I have changed—I am a woman! I have been exposed to the graces and wiles of the world. Why does he cling to his illusion? I've given up mine—why can't he?" A transformation had, indeed, taken place. It had changed the shy, sweet girl into a statuesque, graceful, and beautiful woman of twenty-three. She had grown as hard as some men in her thinking during the critical year past—the year of her return from the courts of Europe. Each day, she seemed to grow more unyielding in her views.

They were now approaching King Street and Waikiki Road. A bright moon lighted cloudless skies and earth alike. The trees cast huge shadows on the roadway, and the pungent odor of island vegetation reminded her again that Honolulu was truly a large garden where plants and blossoms—pampered in palaces of glass or in the private conservatories of Europe and America—flourished all over the town in a luxuriant, natural state of growth. Her own gardens at Waikiki had become a treasured entanglement of exotic flora.

The smell of an island night! The sea, the cooling trade winds, and vegetation combined to make a pervasive fragrance in the air. She inhaled the sweetness with sensual pleasure. How I love the night-time perfumes of Hawaiian flowers, she thought. The compelling perfumes of some island flowers were released only after dark. These alone would have been enough to bring her out on gallops, night after night. In the long, northern, odorless nights of the winters spent abroad, she would sometimes dream of walking in gardens richly fragrant with blossoms of frangipani, pak lan, pikaki, or aglaia; or dream that she was riding in damp woodlands where mokihana and maile grew, causing the air to be so perfumed as to tantalize one's very being.

On King Street there were roadside lamps at each corner, throwing off a pale yellow light. Her thoughts returned to something she had said during dinner tonight: "It is a strange feeling, Father, to come home after living so many years abroad. I feel like a fish out of the water. I learned to speak French fluently. I speak some German and Italian, and Spanish. I can read proficiently in all these languages. Do you know that there is scarcely any opportunity to use them here? In Europe I could use them continually." She had paused to garner more thoughts after her father had said, rather gruffly under his breath, that she was talking nonsense; that many foreigners landed on these shores; and that from time to time she could have plenty of opportunity to speak French, Italian, or German. He reminded her there was a large colony of Germans in the islands. "And, besides," he had added "it's time you brushed up on your native tongue. Your people expect you to speak Hawaiian." She had! She had "brushed up" on the language of her mother's people. She was becoming more proficient every day in saying particular phrases—even forming sentences. But it was difficult. The native tongue was so full of idioms; its best usage was richly metaphoric, a kind of poetry. How she hoped she might win more understanding from this aging, unhappy man! In mentioning the foreign languages she had learned, she wanted merely to make the point that much of what she had learned abroad was quite irrelevant to living in the islands in the role she now must occupy. How easy it would be if her difficulties could be solved by her speaking Hawaiian fluently!

"Why are you so restless?" her father had asked abruptly, while she searched for words to say something that might give him comfort. His blunt interrogation had dissolved the moment of slight compassion she had felt and had made her say quite angrily: "There are many reasons for my restlessness, but I loathe discussing them again. It seems to me that for ages now, we've talked about little else. I ask you to allow me the privilege of my thoughts—of my own feelings. They are best kept private. I have my horses, my dogs, and the peacocks! Nanny here, and the animals are all the company I want most of the time—except for Koa. He understands more than anyone else my plight. He understands, and he says very little."

Nanny MacDougall, an elderly Scotswoman, her former nurse, now a companion, had listened to these heartbreaking deliberations night after night, a third figure at the great table that once had known abundant hospitality. For long periods now, it offered its burden of fare to only the three people sitting in tense anticipation at its oval boundaries. In her present state of mind, the princess had refused to ask dinner guests to Ainapua; and her father had grown indifferent, even hostile, to most people of the town.

"I have hoped, I have dreamed of your success in life," she remembered the old man saying wistfully, even calmly—spent, for a moment, of the anger that had possessed him a moment ago. "And now you do nothing but waste your time with Koa and the Stevenson girls, talking bitterly about the haoles here."

And he had recalled to her—not for the first time, either—the scene at the wharf when he had gone to welcome her home after the long years she had spent away. What a figure of stately beauty she had been! The wharf had been crowded with flower-bedecked Hawaiians who had come to pay respect to the beautiful young woman, whom some could remember as a shy, wide-eyed, pensive girl who had left her islands to journey across two oceans and a continent nine years earlier when she was only fourteen. The old man had enjoyed a silent triumph on this occasion. His daughter had appeared, that day, to be the very image of regal womanhood. Her courtly nods and bows, her restraint of movement, her fine speech, her well-pitched voice that was displayed as she met various people or as she responded to the loud alohas of the crowd, had illustrated this. Oh how proud, how glowing his spirit had been on that day!

The old man's spoken reverie had softened her. She had smiled and said that it had been one of the happiest days of her life. Then she had remembered his reference to Prince Kealiikoa and the Stevenson girls. "Why shouldn't we talk about the haoles, Father? They took our government away from us," she had said with a bitter laugh. "Besides," she had continued without relaxing her bitterness, "they are so unctiously censorious! You would think everyone here should scrape and bow to their wishes. What ungrateful people they are! My Hawaiian ancestors were extremely kind to the ancestors of those people when they came here! And their thanks was to be cruelly critical of everything Hawaiians believed in. How ungrateful and how disrespectful!"

Recollection of this last fragment of the talk at dinner made her restive. She loosened her grip on the reins and urged Damozel into a slow trot; but soon she brought the horse again to a walk. She disliked converting annoyance into a physical act. "Good girl, Damozel! Good, good girl! You are indeed an Arab princess!" One could love animals inordinately, she thought.

Quite suddenly she became conscious of a smell from the sea. The delicious fragrance calmed her. South winds, having disturbed the tides and currents, causing seaweed to be torn from the coral reef, blew the piquant fragrance to the shore. She was on King Street, quite far from the sea, riding toward town, yet the air was heavy with the smell of li-poa. The smell of limu li-poa was unmistakable—like no other. Li-poa! It was primordial, indigenous—a dry and full-flavored seaweed. Rough seas had torn the frizzy yellowish strands from their pinions on the coral and washed them to the shore. Having lived in Waikiki through all her childhood years, the princess knew well the smell of li-poa.

Limu li-poa! How could one forget words attached to such a fragrance? The senses were a powerful influence on the fabric of memory. Other seaweed names were more elusive—they were not easily etched into memory; but they were charmingly descriptive: hulu-hulu aina (a hairy seaweed), aala-ula (a piquant one), or limu ele-ele (green and silky) which the Hawaiians ate with beef stew.

"Easy, Damozel! Smell the limu, you English Arab! Smell the limu!"

The prolonged winters in England had not numbed all the senses that related her to the earlier years when her mother and certain retainers had repeated the spoken lore of her Polynesian ancestors. She had not forgotten the familiar sounds—the words tossed from ancient lips so musically and with such intrinsic veneration for the age-old textures of legend and epic. In spite of certain maneuvers from her earliest childhood to remove her from native speech and influences, living circumstances had interceded and made their imprint on her mind. How could she forget the somber talk of aged retainers, or the joyous exclamations of the younger fold, or the soft exchanges of conversation between her mother, Aunt Lydia, and Uncle David.

Mountain ranges and waterfalls, flowers—gaudy and fragrant—the mountain ferns, towering spreading trees as primordially indigenous as her mother's ancestors bore the beautiful names of the language. Fish and land animals, the sky, or a vista from the dizzy heights of a cliff, the burnished earth of volcanic craters...the sad, lingering sounds of death-wailing, the small pastel-colored native birds, the roster of native gods and goddesses . . . there were words in the music of the native tongue to describe by name all of these.

She could remember most of them. The smell of ginger flowers recalled awapuhi: the primitive half-wail and half-chant of grief-showing recalled the unforgettable kani-kau. The names of massive, brown ancestors—some of them as descriptively individual as the names given mountains, the sea, and the heavens: Keohokalole, Keawe-heulu, Kekaulike, Kamanawa, or Kapaakea—these she did not forget. Old Kali, the devoted butler at Ainapua, had ingrained them into her memory, giving her expert and furtive instruction when Nanny MacDougall or her father were not close by. Kali, with the gift that some Hawaiians have for genealogical remembrance, could recite the names of the princess's ancestors, going many generations into the past.

These names were in the heart—they brought up the sounds of words and a shower of associations from the deepest recesses of memory. They were the roots of ancestry and race, of one part of her. She could not forget them. They were a part of her in a more classic setting, in a romantic backward-looking way. She associated them with what she knew of indigenous times—the times of feather-cloaked chiefs, their impressive height so dramatized by tall feather-covered helmets—some of whom could still be seen along lonely mountain ridges or deep in hidden valleys.

But this poetic view of the language had not created her a Hawaiian in the contemporary sense. She could not join her people in the margins of their present world, one made of telephones, locomotives, banks, concrete and brick buildings, and heavily populated city slums for masses of her people. I cannot speak to them in our native tongue, she thought bitterly. I am, therefore, a Hawaiian only to the extent that intellect and imagination link me romantically to the past. How cruel! How confusing life can be, when you think of all these things. "Yes, Damozel, yes! It is all quite confusing, but we cannot wish such things out of their places in the mind. We are doomed to think of them—to make sense of them!"

Tea and cakes, refined elocution, the restrained niceties of genteel deportment, the charm of a delicate ball dress, the waltz, the comforting camaraderie of county fairs, the elegance of Adam and Temple drawing rooms with their Hepplewhite and Sheraton furnishings or the fashionable grace of Sir Joshua's or Gainsborough's ladies, had captured her fancy, too, and she would not soon erase them from memory or from the very core of her being. They, too, were a part of the complex fabric of heritage and culture.

But they were only a part. The other part of her drew its substance from aboriginal Polynesian sources; and of this she was fully conscious. Urgings and promptings from the archetype repository fashioned some of her impulses—some of her feelings—which no amount of intellection could destroy.

The princess had not realized until her return from the long years abroad that two great streams of influence gave fierce battle within her for supremacy over feelings and thoughts. The temptation to plunge headlong into the vast comforting arms of nature—made the less resistible by endless sunshine, fragrant trade wind breezes, and the delicious purity of her island waters—continually haunted her splendid body.

There had been Captain Beautemps. Now there was Koa. "Koa, Kealiikoa! How beautiful even his name! The Noble Soldier!" How handsome he was, and how the grace of the Polynesian showed in his walk, his voice, his manner. "Shake your head, little Arab princess, I know you agree," she said to her horse, and laughed. Oh how comforting the night was, how pleasantly neutral was the less obvious physical completeness of things in the darkness. *Do I love Koa?* In truth she could not answer this. She admired him; she respected him. "I am two people," she said to herself and Damozel, "I am a house divided!"

At times she would have joined the women in their squidding, spear fishing or gathering limu in the shallows of Ala Moana and Waikiki. In the coverings of her stately gowns, she watched them at these pursuits in the sea, jealous to be as anonymous and free as they. Everything she did was held under the scrutiny of watching eyes, and talked about. So innocent a thing as gathering limu or fishing would have lifted eyebrows. "She is going native, returning to the old ways," the watchful, anxious, critical ones would say.

At other times, perhaps, as she remembered reading the letters of

Madame de Sevigne, or the Journal of the Duchess of Newcastle, squidding and fishing in the native way would have repulsed her; for civilization had also made its claims on her, and, laying claims to her education and knowledge, she would have been called "pretentious," "uppity!" A soft, decorative nonentity was what some desired her to be. Actually, she was two people, and in this was the seed of her torment. *Who am I? What am I?* she had asked herself with a monotonous regularity.

She had gathered together a narrow circle of friends, mostly half-whites like herself, and retreated to the cottage at Ainapua. It had been an elaborate child's playhouse, built especially for her. It was lost now among thickets of palms with exotic and cumbersome names. Her father had altered the cottage, made it larger, and refurbished it to celebrate her return from England. Here she could retire with her friends and be herself. They would sing and talk, though for some reason she was never at ease. "My handful of friends are very kind to me—and they understand to some extent. They certainly have greater understanding than my father, and they try to make me feel at home again in Hawaii. I appreciate their solicitations, and I try to shake off those influences eight years of living in Europe has etched on my soul which interfere with my feeling at home in Hawaii," she had written her close friend, the Honorable Hermione Paget, now the Marchioness of Tindale. She had earnestly devoted herself to knowing what it meant to be a Hawaiian again. Koa had told her: "You are so English, Victoria! So stiff and formal! And your words come out in freshets, full of brilliance and keenness. You leave us far behind!" Why does he say such a thing? It is too candid, too intimate! "But, Koa," she had answered, almost sternly, "I am Hawaiian, and I'm proud of the fact!" He had said nothing, and looked at her gently as they walked in the garden, followed by the peafowl and the dogs.

Days on end, she had walked the luxuriant gardens of the estate at Waikiki, followed by her mother's peacocks and the greyhounds that she had brought from England—committed forever now to fulfill their days in warmer air, amidst palms and ferns rather than in the cool dark woods of England. Days of walking along the twisting, softly curling pathways of the famous gardens, restraining tears, erasing thoughts, flashing irrelevancies into consciousness to blot out painful memory. Days of walking to escape the shadows gathering in her mind; to elude the pounding thrusts of ennui and the sense of defeat that was so great she had to constantly warn herself against giving in to despair.

Both the bitches she had brought from England had whelped; there was now a small army of greyhounds at Ainapua who were constantly in attendance during these walks in the garden. When Koa was not there, Nanny MacDougall would sometimes join her. A wily psychologist, Nanny had used these more reflective and poignant moments to influence the princess away from the elegiac direction her thoughts had taken. "Think, my dear, of Marie Antoinette, or Mary of the Scots! They lost their heads!" Although the old nurse's rather melodramatic offering of consolation had amused Victoria, she had felt grateful for it.

Perversely, darkness and its balmy air could somehow ease the parasitic draw of melancholy. She let herself feel, again and again, the peaceful neutrality of night as she rode the Arabian mare along King Street. She walked the horse for several blocks before urging her into a gallop again. Before they reached the Palace and Aliiolani Hale, she turned Damozel toward Punchbowl Street. She had vowed never to enter the Palace again. It had become a source of pain even to drive by the stylish domicile, converted as it was into an office building, where the bearded, pale-eyed president of the so-called republic and his staff had their offices. There were too many associations with her girlhood at the sight of the square colonnaded building that resembled some of the newer villas she had seen in Europe. She eased the little mare into a trot when they reached Vineyard Street, several blocks above the Palace, and turned left into the darkness.

Then she remembered more words her father had spoken. Stubbornly, they crowded her thoughts. "Your people need you now, more than ever, my dear! They need a symbol of leadership, even if the government and the throne are lost. You fit the specifications. You have been trained for this," her father had said.

"To fit into the role of a royal has-been? This is all that is left, Father? I am only the former heiress apparent to the Hawaiian throne. Should I assume this role, and conduct myself accordingly—as a tractable has-been?"

"This house, this garden, I have raised them from the mud flats to create a home befitting a princess," her father had said with a sadness. "You can be the reigning lady of the land—without the throne. I will leave money enough—enough for you to be completely independent!"

"Will money dispel loneliness? After the years of study and travel, of cautious and extensive training to command as mine the things of civilization—the theater, the music, the wit and cleverness of educated people—do you think I can easily come back here to melt wistfully into the role you specify for me? To queen it over a little circle of shopkeeper's wives, or the handful of wellborn Hawaiians and hapa-haoles who are already as broken in spirit and demoralized as I? Please,

Father, allow me the privacy of my bitterness—my own sense of futility!"

"This is weakness! You are being self-indulgent! Your warrior ancestors and the bold Scots from whom you descend through me would growl with rage to hear you talk this romantic nonsense. No, Victoria, no! You have a life here of great importance. You still live in the hearts of your people us their princess—as Aunt Lydia is still their queen!"

"This is lofty talk, Father, but does it really provide the answer for me? With the risk of being repetitive and dull—even sentimental—I might say again, you are destroying what happiness I might have by taking so critical an attitude of Koa. First of all, you were critical of Captain Beautemps!"

"He would not have made a suitable husband here."

"Why not? You married Mother—weren't you a suitable husband here?"

"It was different. I had lived here for many years before I married your mother. We were both close to the scene. Captain Beautemps would have come here uninitiated. He would not have known how to take things."

She had wanted to say some harsh cruel thing about her father's present attitude toward Prince Kealiikoa, but she had suppressed it. Words seemed quite valueless at that moment. Damozel shied as a prowling cat streaked across the road in front of them.

"What about Adam Pierce? He's a fine young man!" her father had demanded. Recalling this statement at the moment the horse shied, the princess was nearly thrown. "Yes, Father, absolutely to your specifications!" As she struggled to keep her seat, the words tumbled into her mind. "A perfect match, on your terms, now! He has a promising future in business, and with my assets to pump life into his efforts at accumulating money, he could become quite rich someday!"

Her father's reaction had been to send up a barrage of questions. Where had his daughter learned to think so vulgarly? When had the delicacy of the girlhood mind turned to take this direction of manlike awareness—of intensive knowing? "You talk at times like a man!" he had said accusingly.

He had had her trained to rule! Was this a man's mind? She had been trained to lead and plan for her people. Some of the world's great rulers had been women. Was it a man's mind that was required to rule a nation, to deal with rulers of other nations? What about the great Queen Elizabeth? Maria Theresa? Catherine of Russia? Man's mind? "I have been taught to think, Father—to use intellect as an instrument of survival in specific circumstances. I was trained to rule someday as a queen. That destiny has been taken from me. So now, intellect becomes ironically the instrument of my distress, my doom! What else can I be now but a soured malcontent?"

"You can be a woman, and a princess! A living symbol of the chiefs of old!"

Then he had taken another approach in the effort to penetrate the hard surface of her present thinking, and he asked: "Just what are your intentions with Prince Koa? I've watched you when he has come here. You seem quite indifferent—even bored. Perhaps you really do share my feelings that marrying him would be a mistake. You are rich, and he is not. You are a sophisticated, intelligent woman of superior training. He is just a good-natured island boy!"

"So Prince Kealiikoa is 'just a good-natured island boy,' and I am neither fish nor fowl—neither queen, nor just another citizen. I am ex-officio heiress apparent to the little throne here! I am now, to put it rather bluntly, a walking anachronism!" Again, the unwomanly words, not becoming the rare and delicate flower that had been enshrined in her father's mind before her return from England! Her words had thrust deep, and, knowing this, she had gone on: "Prince Koa is a good friend, and certain things about me he understands. He is kind, and he has warmth. I cannot see now where marriage is the issue!"

"What about children?" her father countered.

"Please, Father, be a little merciful! I haven't the heart to bear children who might suffer what I've had to endure for the past five years. Our wanderings abroad!" she had said almost savagely. "For more than three years, we were kept away from here by the people who seized the throne. They were afraid that I, of all people, would foment trouble! My presence might bring on a revolution, they said. I cannot forget the anguish of those years, the terrible longing to be here where I was born, and had a place! And now, the humiliation and dishonor of having to be stared at as a royal has-been. Children! Such a thing is in God's hands. My own thoughts on the matter are quite harsh and conclusive!"

"You seem to have no aim in life—no desire for some established end," her father had said. "You seem to be sleepwalking most of the time. Are you so tired of life already?" It was as though no word of her outpouring of the truth of her plight had penetrated to her father. He had accepted all her losses—why couldn't she? "No, Victoria, no! You can have a good life here. You have a place of endearment in the hearts of your people!"

"Yes, Father, I can be an object of sentiment—perhaps even an object of pity. Remember the official portrait that was made in London before I left? I was in my soft, silken, primrose-yellow gown. Worth, who dressed all the royal ladies of Europe, designed it for me to wear to the ball given by the Prince of Wales and Alexandra. Let the people have that picture to soothe their broken hearts. It's as much as I have. And, anyway, it is a fine photograph!"

The words were harsh, rasping, and, in some respects, she knew they were unbecoming. Koa, too, had said to her only the other day: "You talk and think like a man! Sometimes I can't follow you!" She had failed to make her father understand that his view of her was a romantic idealization. Would it be the same with Koa? Her true self was locked in her most private thoughts and feelings. These she could not share with anyone.

Sometimes only a thin thread of music came into her mind—something from a chorale or a mass—she knew not which. And other times she heard the sounds of marching armies; and she would say, *Fight! Fight! Take up arms, people of Hawaii*! At other times she heard again the deep but fragile voice of the old Queen at Windsor saying: "You are a pretty child, my dear, and you are my namesake. What a pretty child you are, indeed!"

In her reflections, she would try to sort out the facts—remove her own feelings from influencing what she could make of the holocaust that had ended Hawaiian Monarchy and ushered in what was now a fait accompli: annexation to the United States. She questioned Koa, her father, and one or two older women of their set, about what had happened in 1893. They said one thing or another, but restively indicated their distaste for the subject. "It's all over now. Let us be at peace with ourselves and the new order," was her father's favorite reply.

The accusations aimed at her uncle, the now-deceased Kalakaua Rex, and at the ex-Queen—were they true? Could Uncle David have been so profligate, so comic in his maneuvers? Could Aunt Lydia have been so stubborn, so inept in her rule, as they had reported? *They!* She thought accusingly of the handful of whites who now controlled the economic life of the islands, who had been the main force behind the destruction of the Hawaiian throne. How I loathe them—the shoddy ingrates! They speak of democracy! I have read their constitution—the one created for the Republic of Hawaii. It is more authoritarian and reactionary than any that existed here before. It is a monument of bluestocking arrogance! They destroy a monarchy that was benign and one that provided them with all their opportunities to get rich. They take control of the government, and create an oligarchy, and make laws far less generous to the peoples of this land. They even took the vote away from most Hawaiians by establishing property qualifications which could not be met. We were landless and without money. Most of us lived in poverty in our own homeland.

They would say that, as whites, they had a distaste for living in our beautiful islands and being ruled by dark-skinned people. That is something they will never admit, for they are so unctious! So cruelly vindictive! They are the kind of haoles that have gone out all over the world and enslaved people who do not have white skins.

The ex-princess sedulously avoided confronting these people. Their mealy-mouthed expressions of goodwill were insincere, revolting! These were her legacy of thought, for no one had told her, to any informative degree, just what had happened in 1893—not even Koa. Her knowledge of the details was scant. The ex-Queen, Liliuokalani, one of the chief characters of the tragedy, was absent from Honolulu at the time of Victoria's return. In letters from Washington, her Aunt Lydia advised she would learn of the trouble of 1893 in a book the ex-Queen was writing, one in which she hoped to relate in detail the events of the overthrow from her own point of view. Her father, not wanting to burden his daughter—his precious flower of regal womanhood—had come forth with the most peremptory statements about the upheaval which had ended Hawaiian sovereignty. There seemed to be a conspiracy at large in the islands to spare Victoria the full story of her aunt's dethronement.

"You must act with restraint now, my daughter. You must be cautious and discreet," her father once had said a few days after her return from England. "Your trip to Washington with Mr. Thorpe to plead the cause of the monarchy didn't set well with the conquerors. They will watch your every move!"

"I made the trip to Washington when I was seventeen, because I felt it was my business to plead for the cause of our government. These are *our* islands. *Our* people have ruled over them for centuries. Why shouldn't I have gone to Washington to plead for the cause of monarchy?"

Yes, and letters and news items had appeared frequently in newspapers, making shabby attempts to humiliate her—to force upon her in a crude schoolboyish way an acceptance of things as they were—after she had paid the official visit to Washington with Mr. Thorpe. She had laughed heartily at the inept phrasing, the downright vulgarity, exhibited in the newspaper bits, which she had received in letters from Nanny MacDougall. They had reflected such provincialism and such ignorance—really! Had graciousness and style already begun to depart from the island scene? she had thought after receiving one envelope full of clippings.

From the miasma of thoughts that went back to the past, as she rode tonight, one memory called forth the image of a pale emaciated face. It belonged to a tall wraith of a man who wore his hair carelessly tossed and long. He was so thin, so pale. Day after day, in the weeks before she left for England, he had come to Ainapua to talk with her father. Having settled comfortably into the large fan-backed chairs on the verandah, they had talked. Some meaning of the words had escaped her; yet enough was understood to know that the famous man of letters and her father exchanged ideas on the subject of local politics. There was an intensity in their words, a jarring note of alarm. A certain faction was asking for changes in the government; and, every day, attacks had been made publicly and privately upon the King. Poor Uncle David—he was not a gifted statesman, but he was able! He worked as hard as anyone in the government! Why had they judged him so harshly, called him those awful names, and cast aspersions, of all things, on his parentage? All this had happened so long ago. It belonged to another dimension of her consciousness—a time when she was innocent and fourteen. At the time, she could only feel in her child's heart a sense of alarm—an elusive and delicately poised sense of alarm which children feel when they overhear some things adults say. The talk of the gifted visitor and her father was sprinkled with words like "annexation" and "manifest destiny," "white supremacy" and "ungrateful haoles."

Some words the gifted man had written her when she left Hawaii stayed fast in her memory over the years. She easily recalled: "When she comes to my land, her father's, and the rain beats upon the window (as I fear it will), let her look at this page: it will be like a weed, gathered and pressed at home; and she will remember her own islands, and the shadow of the mighty trees; and she will hear the peacocks screaming in the dusk and the wind blowing in the palms; and she will think of her father sitting there alone."

Uncertainty, and a cool and relentless sense of outrage at what had happened in Hawaii during her absence, made her loath to see or speak to some who had formerly been friends. It hurt all the more to ignore them as carriages passed on the roadways, or they met in someone's drawing room, because they were so familiar. She was fourteen when she had left Hawaii—an age when the memory of those one has known for a lifetime is forever etched in the tissues of remembrance. In public, these feelings of outrage were particularly tormenting as she could not exhibit vexation when on view to the world.

And so she had ridden on, in wild galloping spurts that would be reduced to slow trotting and then to a walk. On Vineyard Street, Victoria on her Arabian mare passed the house in which she had made her royal entrance into the world. It was occupied now by a rich Hawaiian grande dame and her four half-white daughters of extraordinary beauty. It was a lovely house with a square turret in the middle, looming above the porte cochere. She remembered going up to the turret with Kali to hang the Hawaiian flag from a white pole that shot out at an angle. Her father had built the larger house at Ainapua before her mother's death. They had been living there a number of years before Victoria was sent to England. She loved the house, and paid its darkened form a long, respectful, studious look as she rode by, remembering that her mother had planted some of the trees that now had reached great height and swayed above in the darkness.

After crossing Queen Emma Street, she saw the mansion of the old Princess Deborah, which now had been converted into a public high school. Princess Deborah had deeded the land at Waikiki to Victoria on the day she was born. Had Deborah known wild defiance; and had she known heartache and the vitiating sting of defeat? It would have been impossible. No one—no one at all—had told Deborah that there were do's and do not's, that there was this restraint or that restraint to be exercised. She had moved through life with the instinctual force and wisdom of an elephant. She had torn from the cake of life large hunks for herself, and swallowed them triumphantly. A flash of recollection brought forth the memory of superbly-gowned women and courtly men dancing long into the night. Their laughter and talk now filled Victoria's ears, and she smiled. Nothing could have stopped the massive chiefess from enjoying life—except death, itself, which had visited her mercifully before the predatory ones had seized the throne. She was so bent on pleasure, and wise and strong, as well.

But the old Princess Deborah had left no children to continue the family line. Her heir, a cousin, had also died childless, leaving the great house to the restrained New Englander she had married. It seemed to be a condition of Hawaiian royalty in these times to be quite childless. Victoria's own aunt, the ex-Queen, was without issue, as was the Dowager Queen Kapiolani. The Princess Harieta Nahienaena, the daughter of the great Kamehameha, had died childless at twenty-two, surrendering to heartbreak and debauchery. The Princess Victoria Kamamalu had died at twenty-six, also childless and victim of a similar capitulation.

Why had all this happened? Why? she asked herself with vehemence. What had happened to her race that its most patrician representatives could no longer reproduce themselves? A melancholy fact that pointed up the irrefutable, disheartening specter of decline among her people. In the old days, royal children were numerous. She let a sigh escape. The mare picked up her ears. "It's nothing, Damozel, nothing! I am only thinking about some tragic facts." Why? She could no more erase consciousness of these sad losses than she could wishfully change the color of her dark brown eyes. She had been trained to think; to ponder; to evaluate.

After this, she had trotted Damozel up Fort Street, oppressed and heavy under the weight of the nostalgic interlude. I must stop giving in to these depressing looks backward that every landmark readily summons to my mind.

Near School Street, surrounded by spreading gardens, the house of a rich and prominent part-white family came into view. She thought of the dark-eyed, dark-haired children, who lived here—somewhat overdressed, somewhat overprotected, and idealized—as she had been. Would they ever know her torment and her sense of loss? Or would time and the ruthless propensity of the life force change the order of things and create, from future circumstances, a world better suited for these children to grow up in? Hauteur and fashion belonged to their parents. They had held a firm and glamorous place at the social peak of the kingdom. They owned land and cattle, carriages and beautiful horses. Was this enough? Was it enough to have incomparable physical beauty, to be clothed in splendid uniforms and gorgeous holokus; to own lands, carriages, and fine horses? Was it enough to walk with astonishing dignity; to breed an unyielding pride that separated them sharply from all other people?

"Pride goeth before the fall!" She had heard this oft repeated in Victorian England—and here! Was this stiff pride that was so common to aristocratic Hawaiians and part-Hawaiians a natural thing or was it bravado—a system of defense against any encroachment of white supremacy attitudes upon their lives? "White supremacy!" she growled at the darkened air.

This was really the basis of her father's dislike of Koa. She was now quite certain of this. Her father could marry a native and beget a child; he was a man! White men could marry native women; never the reverse. With her education and travels, her father perhaps saw her as a white woman—certainly she had been trained like one. "Oh, Koa, Koa," she whispered. "Oh, Koa!"

She patted the mare's beautifully arching neck to gain reassurance.

The little horse snorted sympathetically. After they passed Kuakini Road, the fleet animal broke into a canter, and then a full gallop, as though an intuitive communication existed between herself and her mistress. The princess wanted at that moment to force Damozel into a furious gallop. But there had been no need to dig the heels of her boots into the mare's flanks; nor had it been necessary to work her into the chase with the usual verbal encouragements. Without being urged in the slightest, Damozel flew up the ascending road that narrowed perceptibly as it meandered more deeply into the valley.

Rain began to fall as they entered the lonely stretch above Hanaiakamalama. It was not a heavy rain—more like a thickened mist, and it did not discourage the princess and her horse. They flew on, to the furthermost reaches of the valley. The area was heavily wooded and unspoiled by habitations.

At Mamalahoa the frizzy mist turned into rain—a heavy, cold, upper Nuuanu rain. Still the beauteous rider and the dappled mare galloped on. How luxuriant were the smells here! Wild nature—unspoiled, unexpurgated; budding and leafing, flowering and ripening; decaying leaves, twigs, blooms in brown masses formed thick layers of compost under shrub and tree; kukui trees and ferns—pulu, pala palai, ho-io made the more fragrant with the fall of rain—grew in profusion here. The ferns were another link with the deep past. They had been celebrated, time and again, in the ancient meles, the epics of classic Hawaii which were preserved by people remembering them word for word. She reined Damozel to a stop. She studied the world around her—even in the rain and mist it was breathtaking.

This was Koa's world. It was his favorite place to come on rides. A mystical calm would come over his face when they rode, as they sometimes did, to this point in the valley. He would recite pieces of the ancient chants and translate them. He would become a chief of the old days, surveying his domain. Within this romantic framework, his eyes shining, his face aglow with hope, he seemed so far away—drawn back deep into a time of simplicity and calm that was far, far out of her reach. But tonight it was her world as well. It belonged to her as well as to Koa. The beating rain, primordial fragrances, and the clean wind chased away the specters of sorrow. She felt a surge of pure delight fill her being. She was freed from the heat of anger and outrage, from the dread feelings of doubt and confusion that had so relentlessly plagued her recent existence.

The mare's delicate feet found comfortable grooves between the rounded paving stones—her gait was even: a fast walk.

The smells. The shadows. The dripping foliage, How glorious is this island world of Hawaii nei, the princess mused. And here in the upper woodlands the Wa'o Kuahiwi. Nuuanu—it is our world—it does not belong to the foreigners. Without warning, the stately, cool and rigidly controlled Victoria began to cry. She sobbed in the shameless, earthy way of a chiefess of old in moments of sorrow. The horse responded with nervous reflexes of her neck and shoulder muscles.

"It's all right Damozel," she cried out, "I need to cry—I have not cried since we returned." The tears gushed out and little rivulets ran down her cheeks to the sides of her mouth. The salty moisture of her grief mixed with the sweetness of rain drops pelting her face. She felt relief well up as she let the tears escape the confines of her famously beautiful eyes.

At first the sound of the drums was barely audible. Gradually, it grew louder.

Damozel reared, nearly throwing her. The frenzied horse snorted wildly and reared again and then once again—what on earth is happening to you—you English Arab?

The horse sidled first to one side of the roadway then another—the drum beats became louder.

"What is happening?" she screamed and then called out, "Koa. O, Koa where are you? Something is happening here which I cannot understand."

The moon broke through clouds rushing over Nuuanu Valley toward the sea. The rain had stopped. The winds blew away in other directions. It had stopped raining. Now she could hear the dry, hollow sound of gourds and calabashes striking one another. In a moment it was clear. She was at the fringe of what she had heard described by her mother's retainers as huakai no ka po. These were the marchers of the night. The dead of old Hawaii who marched on the night of Kane, po Kane, on treks to revels or to sacred rituals.

"Po Kane!" she said under her breath. "What shall I do?" Pale yellow circles of light were approaching, the flickering kukui torches reflecting the procession at the head of which were the proud chiefs of old in splendid cloaks of red and yellow feathers. Alongside them their massive chiefesses, adorned with golden feather leis and other exquisite personal decoration. All wore the lei niho palaoa, the carved whale tooth held upright by hundreds of strands of braided human hair. Warriors and retainers and the kahunas in white tapa draped at an angle across their shoulders accompanied the chiefs, followed by women and children in the simpler garb of farmers and fishermen, bearing gourd and calabash containers.

She was dazed now and blindly accepting the scene. It would not be erased. "I will let happen what will. Whatever it is," she groaned, feeling a pang of fear enter her stomach like a dagger's thrust. Koa had told her of these Nuuanu night marches. He had heard and seen them. His mother, the Princess Kekaulike, was famed for her knowledge of the old lore. Her retainers had passed on some of this wisdom of the ancient culture to Prince David, her eldest son.

The marchers were surely the Oahu alii slain by the dreaded Kahekili of Maui. She recalled the image of this king—a man seven feet tall, one half of his body tattooed in black squares to terrorize his foes in battle. He turned his eyelids inside out with the use of bamboo slits; yet he was famed among his people as a poet and philosopher. The father of the great Kamehameha. A strange man. Why did he devote so many years of his life to the destruction of Oahu's culture—covetous of its attainments and bountiful wealth? He had practically succeeded in decimating the highest-ranking families of Oahu. She shuddered remembering their bones—Elani's, Kanamanu's, Kalaki's, Pupuka's, set up in the dread House of Bones in Moanalua.

"They march on the night of Kane. They march in this valley—in all the valleys," Koa had told her one day as they rode to the pali. He had not dreamed she would ride here alone at night.

The mare grew more skittish. She trembled. Her graceful legs were hardly able to move because of the trembling.

"Go on girl," Victoria urged. "Go on—we won't be stopped by this—it's all right. I know what is happening."

It was then she starkly realized that the entire procession walked a foot or two above the ground. Her spirit froze. Her skin was now a lava waste of lumps brought on by fear. She reined in the Arab.

I shall wait.

Unexpectedly, two chiefs broke the ranks of the procession and stood silently, confronting her. She rose in her saddle. Sat stiffly in defiance.

"He wahine alii Hawaii—owau nei—" she shouted.

"Keiki hua owau—Kepookalani, Aikanaka, Kamanawa, Kamaekalani, Kameeiamoku, Kamehameha nui—" she shouted all the names of ancestors she could remember.

One name came through the mist of time. She had remembered somewhere in her genealogy a marriage to the royal house of Oahu.

"Kaneikaiwilani" she said with authoritative firmness— remembering he was of the royal house of Oahu who married her great-ancestress Queen Keakealani. Victoria came down from the sacred Princess Kalanikauleleiaiwi, a daughter of that union.

The chiefs stood in silence. Two of the kahunas approached and commanded. "Leave her alone. She is one of ours. Leave her alone and continue the march." They waved their carved sticks with dog-tail brushes in the direction of the Princess.

For a few moments she seemed to be unconscious. When she awakened the marchers were gone; their drum beats could no longer be heard. The horse stood quietly now and the wind returned. "On we go, you nervous little creature of the desert sands. How do you like what we have just seen? Do such miraculous things take place in Arabia? Certainly not Beretania where they drink all that tea!"

They proceeded at a fast walk.

When she reached the Pali, she dismounted, walked to the edge of the cliff, and gazed into the vast darkness below. The wind was blowing with particular force. It sent huge swirls of fog and rain billowing over the famous precipice, making it impossible for her to loiter at the edge. She remembered lines from the great epic *Pele and Hiiaka*. This had been her goal for the night; and she had reached it. There was no further significance to her being here alone and at such an unprecedented hour. The common belief that certain timeless supernatural essences were the masters of the Pali at midnight and the early morning hours had not inhibited her desire to come here. And now some lines of the beautiful Pele and Hiiaka saga came to her. Hiiaka, the graceful and beautiful younger sister of the volcanic goddess, who alone among Pele's sister's offered to make the strenuous journey from Hawaii to Kauai to induce handsome Prince Lohiau to return with her and be joined in love to Pele.

How splendidly and beautifully had Hiiaka sung of the beauties of the Koolau, the windward side of Oahu. The hula dancers of Victoria's mother, Likelike, were noted for their performances of this saga. It had made her Uncle David jealous that his younger sister had been able from her youthful training in Kealakekua to be so steeped in the ancient lore she could inspire her chanters and dancers to perform with near perfection.

She remembered a fragment:

Ino Koolau, e, ino Koolau!
Ai kena i ka ua o Koolau!

Half-smiling she whispered, "How far away I've gone from all of this my birthright. How far—I ka puolo waimaka o ka onihi ke kulu iho nei, e."

My eyes a bundle of tears,
Are full to overflowing.

The words soothed. She stopped crying. She stood at the edge of the famous cliff and lifted her arms to the sky, to the towering mountain above her—Lanihuli—Heavens turned upside down. The rain and wind had stopped again. In the distance Kualoa, Moku-lii and the bastion walls of the Koolau Range were all visible in the moonlight. Willful perversity had started her riding in the dark; and on this particular night it had carried her here, far from the comfortable boundaries of her estate at Waikiki; "Papa and Wakea my progenitors I am here—I am yours," she cried out loudly.

She felt a glorious surge of freedom—of being at peace with everything. Arbitrary restraints, the ponderous burden of position and responsibility—the whole struggle of being at odds with life in the land of her birth—all suddenly dissolved, leaving her weary and confused spirit refreshed and cleansed. She mounted her horse, and started upon the long, wet ride home.

Victoria recalled words from the great Kumulipo chant of creation—the words Uncle David and her mother and Aunt Lydia had been at times so frantic in their efforts to remember.

"Darkness of the sun, darkness of the night. Nothing but night. O ka lipo o ka la, o ka lipo o ka po—po wali ho-i." She chanted the words—first in English and then in Hawaiian on the ride back to Waikiki.

It was almost dawn when the servants and Nanny MacDougall heard the clatter of Damozel's hooves on the main drive. It was drizzling in Waikiki. Her father had slept through the hub-bub resulting from the sight of her return. She was drenched and tired—so was the mare—from the long ride, the exposure to the rains. A chill and fever had already begun to exact a toll on her strong young body. She had fallen on the verandah near the heavy front doors, and it was there that Nanny and Kali found her. In two week's time, she would be dead.

Olga Kaupiko's Treasure

It was a crying shame, the way some of these old Hawaiians carried on. They never seemed to tire of certain pleasures. Give them a bowl of poi, a gallon of wine, a pot of stew, and somebody they could make love to—and away they went for as long as food and drink and desire held out.

"Sickening, just sickening," Pauline Irwin hissed to the lattices around her *lanai*, the sitting porch at the back of her house.

Old Maka was celebrating her seventy-fifth birthday. In her little house, which sat a few feet away, hidden from view by a one-by-twelve board fence which separated Pauline Irwin from her neighbors at the rear, the celebration had made a sinful and raucous progress into its third day. Singing and dancing, frequent fights, and certain marathonic amorous adventures had taken place along with the consuming of several gallons of Tokay wine, several pots of beef stew, and a goodly number of pounds of poi.

Pauline Irwin had sat alone in her old house, tormented with the desire to call the police from the moment the first loud noises had issued from the back cottage three days before.

The party was bursting into song again, a lewd suggestive song surviving from the old days:

"*Hau'alii tamuena la, moi tahaua la*"

Shameful! All of Pauline's training at the Episcopal School for Girls, the Priory, in Honolulu of the old days, made her revolt against nonsense of this kind.

She cursed her Aunt Emma for buying her this house in the heart of what had become, over the years, the proletarian stronghold of Kalihi; and now, because things had gone bad and she was reduced to living on the pittance that an annuity brought her, she was condemned to live here, right next to the "camp," as the six cottages that sat in two rows of three houses each were called by other inhabitants of the neighborhood.

The old folks would be turning in their graves, Pauline mused fitfully, to hear the kind of things that had wafted out of old Maka's house for the past three days for the whole neighborhood to hear.

The camp had been kept in a state of high ferment since the party began, with neighbors—all of them Hawaiian—streaming in and out of Maka's house in steady waves, to join the nucleus of merrymakers who were Maka's guests from the "Outside." Pauline easily recognized the neighborhood voices above the laughter and singing of the celebrating outsiders. She had heard these voices too often now, in the high pitch of merriment, to mistake their identity.

The life of the camp had known many celebrations over the years, all of them quite drunken even in the dogdays of prohibition. And all of them both a joy and a bane to Pauline Irwin—for she was two people.

One side of her pulled toward the delights of bacchante revelry; the other pulled her feelings into the more icy regions of genteel restraint. In the latter state she was always only a curiosity-bound observer—never totally a participant. A few glasses of wine or two drinks of whiskey made her soar into heights of delicious gaiety; but never did she reach such heights that she forgot that she was once a "Priory girl" in white dimity with ribbons in her hair, or that her name was Irwin: a name that denoted some importance in Hawaii and which categorically set her apart from her riotous neighbors even if she was as poor as they—or poorer!

Never having fully capitulated to the ideals of her training at the Episcopal school, a streak of the pagan had held fast in Pauline's makeup. One whole side of her was as guiltless and as carefree as was old Maka next door.

It was the other side—the side fortified by the Priory training, and the teachings and conscience of her maternal grandfather who had been a Danish count—that made the trouble in Pauline's life. In all fairness, one would be forced to say that it was this more civilized part of her nature, plus congenital asthma, that had brought certain difficulties into her life.

That she had to be censorious of her neighbors' parties was the result of what she called the haole side of her thinking, whites being, to people of Pauline Irwin's generation in Hawaii, highly circumspect in their way of living. This caused deep conflict, for as she was fed from the influences of her other side—her pagan side—she looked upon the censorship of pleasure with utter distaste.

Asthmatic attacks of varying consequence had plagued her from childhood, precluding her from certain activities that are universally enjoyed. Seventeen years of instruction at the old priory school and the chronic asthma had combined wonderfully to aid her in surviving the long years of chastity with tolerable success.

But the pall of spinsterhood had weighed heavily upon Pauline for the past three days as she battled against the impulse to join in the joyous revellings taking place next door, that seemed to grow more enticing with each hour. She had actually begun to itch in her legs, scratching them constantly. This always happened when something excited her.

Old Maka had staggered over three times with the temerity of a fighting cock to ask Pauline to join in the fun. Three times that temerity had met with chilly refusal. The last time Maka had embellished her plea with the promise to Pauline Irwin that a fine soldier boy, "a beeg sahgent," awaited her with open arms, next door.

Just what does she take me for, the old harridan (she had learned the word at the priory school) *telling such a thing! I could hit her on the head with one of my grandmother's poi pounders!* she fumed silently, before telling Maka to go on home to her party. Then she immediately asked for divine forgiveness of her uncharitable thought. *It was still a dirty shame, the way some of these old people presumed things!*

Pauline could not recall that she had ever displayed to old Maka an interest in men. Yet, with incredible audacity, the aging nymphomaniac had used the argument that a man—a big sergeant, the very image of lust itself—waited, willing to bestow his passion upon Pauline, as a lure for her to join the festivities next door.

This sort of thing was enough to make one wonder if there was any sanity left in the world. The old folks, of really olden times, were bawdy—if the stories Pauline had heard about them were true—but she had never heard anything to equal the "cheek" of old Maka.

This wasn't the first time she had attempted to provide Pauline Irwin with a lover. O, no! Several times in the past years she had got herself stirred up over Pauline's state of chaste loneliness. In Maka's eyes, it was a crime for a woman to deny herself the pleasures that only a man can offer. She used Pauline's yard as a short-cut to get to and from the bus that took her to her job in the big laundry downtown; so, twice daily, old Maka had the opportunity to plead her cause on behalf of love to her celibate neighbor.

"You are losing some of the juices of life," the old one would plead in Hawaiian. "One of these days you will no longer be able to enjoy this great gift which the Gods have bestowed upon us!"

The first few times old Maka had made her plea, Pauline had been almost amused. She thought of it as a quaint indication that some of the frankness of the ancients in these matters had survived the sceptically cleansing influences of Calvinist indoctrination. But when it continued, time after time, even after Pauline had rather angrily insisted that such things did not interest her in the least, it became Pauline's conviction that her "leg was being pulled" by old Maka. It was then that she was driven almost to tell the old sinner to stop using her yard as a passageway. Noticing that Pauline was really huhu, angry, old Maka desisted from her pleadings, reminded by Pauline's angry look that being allowed to pass through her garden saved Maka two hundred extra yards of walking to get to and fro from the busline.

It was only when she was quite drunk that she now taunted Pauline with her philosophy of love.

Old Maka would be as meek as a lamb when she came out of this mad flight and had to face up to going back to the steaming mangles or washtubs, or whatever else they used in those big mechanically run laundries downtown. That would be time enough to tell the old hoyden how vile she had been during the past three days. On her way home from the soap and lye and washtubs was the time to give her the devil for this latest piece of insolence.

Deeply lost in these fitful musings, she almost failed to hear Phillip Carysfort's heavy knocking on her front door. When she became fully cognizant of the sound and its significance, she flew to open the door, forgetting that such forceful locomotion could easily bring on a siege of asthma. How she had longed, for the past day or so, for someone to call on her!

"O! Come in my dear, come in! I've been sitting in the back, and didn't hear you knock, at first! How good it is to see you! Mai, mai! Come in, come in!" she said excitedly, her speech broken by intervals of gasping which she tried her best to keep under control. "You have no idea how happy I am to see you! One can be so alone—so lost, really—in this awful neighborhood!" She wheezed piteously, caught her breath, and asked, "What brings you to this part of the world, my dear?"

"I would have telephoned, Aunt Pauline, but since I was so close, I thought I'd just drop in unannounced. I've spent the afternoon at the Bishop Museum."

Phillip Carysfort was fair and of medium height. He was distantly related to Pauline Irwin through his mother. If you knew nothing of his antecedents, it would be difficult to tell that he was part-Hawaiian. An interest in Hawaiiana, which had expanded noticeably since his graduation from college a few years before, had brought him into close friendship with his elderly cousin, Pauline. He had discovered her to be a remarkable informant. She forgot little of what she had ever read, heard, or seen in her sixty years of life. Phillip had found her to be a highly reliable source of information of the more social side of upper-class Hawaiian life around the turn of the century. She remembered names and individuals with surprising clarity, reproducing dead persons by describing in detail their peculiarities of speech and dress, their gestures, or certain other more intimate aspects of their lives.

"Let's go behind. I've been sitting there since I finished my dinner. It seems to be so much cooler back there."

Phillip remembered that certain barnyard odors were always highly prevalent in that part of Pauline's house.

"How are your little feathered friends?" he asked, alluding to the chickens and ducks Pauline kept and sold, at a profit, to supplement her small income.

"O, just fine, just fine. Two of my ducks are setting. One is atop twenty-three eggs. Twenty-three, mind you!"

A peal of shrill laughter came forth from the festive cottage behind the back fence. Clapping and more laughter followed.

"What on earth is that?"

"Don't pay any attention to it! Sheer nonsense, that's all it is. I've been sitting here for the past three days trying to get myself to call the police."

"Sounds as though someone is having a party!"

"Someone is! The old woman behind me—old Maka. You remember her, don't you? Her husband was the old blind man who used to sing for pennies down at the fish market at Aala Park."

"Yes, yes. I do remember," Phillip answered, recalling the old fellow, his guitar, starched dungarees, and clean dress shirts left open at the collar.

"Isn't Maka a bit on in years for this kind of thing?" he asked pointedly.

Again the peals of laughter punctured the soft night air. Someone had begun to sing another lewd song surviving from the past. It spoke of a ship and its sails coming into port, and likened this to the sexual act. Laughter again!

"Someone must be dancing."

"Old Maka thinks she's still sweet sixteen when she does the hula. And, believe me, she doesn't stint on any of the motions," Pauline answered swiftly. Then, as though to erase the words, she said, in a rather loud tone of voice that was out of keeping with the contents of her thoughts, "Would you rather we sat in the front to get away from this noise? I see you've brought your notebooks!"

"O, no. This is fine. We can talk here. I don't mind the party noises."

Pauline had now slipped into a reflective attitude. She could put herself into a reminiscing frame of mind at a moment's notice.

"Have I ever told you the one about the two coconut trees?"

Phillip shook his head and said, "No," quietly, which caused Pauline to reconnoiter the idea speedily.

There were a handful of the old-timers left in town who "kept their eye" on two tall coconut trees in Waikiki. To the uninitiated, or rather, to the uninformed, who passed these trees in legion every day, these two trees were just more of those tall plumed giants that leaned their great waving leaves into the wind. But to the oldsters, who knew, and Pauline was among them, the trees had legendary importance for they marked the ending of a passionate love affair which had begun before Pauline was born.

Before she could muster thoughts and warm up to the telling of the story, another peal of laughter crashed into the decorous stillness of Pauline's house, charging it briefly with a strangely savage irreverence.

"I've listened to that racket back there for three nights!" Pauline's eyes were ablaze with the fires of the righteously indignant.

Phillip Carysfort had come to know his cousin well, of late. He knew that she might express a violent distaste for something, and not feel that way at all at the deeper layers of emotion, as though, on the surface, she was one person in expressing her thoughts on certain prescribed matters, and, underneath, she might be quite someone else with a sentiment the reverse of the one she revealed publicly. He did not allow her last utterance to badger him into aroused concern.

"Has it been so bad?" he asked. "Have there been many fights? Has anyone been hurt?"

"O, mercy!" Pauline bemoaned with a maidenly wail, "There have been several fights. I came damned near to calling the police last night!" She paused and effected the look of penetrating reflection.

"Life in that little camp is certainly a pretty lively affair. If Maka isn't cutting up, you can depend on Lou and Henry to start one of their bloody battles." She coughed a hacking dry cough characteristic of her asthma. "And if it isn't those two who are disturbing the peace of our little neighborhood, then it's the Hanohano family across from Maka."

Pauline brushed straggling, graying hairs away from her jutting prominently-high cheekbones; then her face became possessed of a look of benign sweetness that could only have been fashioned into this expression, this particular pattern, by the memory of a distant pleasure that was now safely cast in the hard and lasting metal of her past.

"This story was told me by an old woman who used to live out at Waikiki. I lived out there, you know, a long time ago with one of my aunts."

Phillip Carysfort sensed the advent of one of Pauline's varied and inimitable reminiscences. He assumed a look of eager expectancy to spur on her talk.

"This old lady, who was a relative of my neighbors next door, the Hanohanos, she told me the story herself. I was a mere girl at the time, scarcely more than eighteen. She was a property owner in old Waikiki. I forget her name except that *Olga* seems to stick in my mind."

"Olga?" Phillip echoed.

"Yes, Olga. O yes, *Olga Kaupiko*. She was an ehu, a red-head. Her people were from Kauai."

"Olga seems an odd name for a Hawaiian woman of her generation!"

"Why so? The Hawaiians were called everything," Pauline chortled. "Why, I even remember one old dear, a huge thing who played the guitar beautifully, whose name was Betty. Betty Maialoha."

"It just struck me that Olga was not a typical name of an old-time Hawaiian woman." Phillip commented further, "But neither is Betty, for that matter."

Pauline was silent.

"Please excuse me for interrupting your story."

He had forgotten for the moment that Pauline Irwin's thoughts were easily diverted, that in a matter of seconds she could leap across mountains and forests of subject matter, spurred on by her kaleidoscope of thoughts.

There was more laughter, cackling laughter, from the house in back but this time it was half-smothered by the strummed music of a guitar and ukulele.

"This Kaupiko woman still talked of her lover as though she were sweet sixteen! Isn't it terrible the way our people dwell on such matters? You would think they had nothing else to talk about to hear some of the old folks carry on!"

She paused to allow a mild attack of choking to pass.

"Olga had a boy friend. He was a commoner. Just one of her husband's kahus, one of his retainers."

Using the habit she had developed in talking with Phillip Carysfort, and other people of his generation, of saying a word in Hawaiian which she immediately translated into English, Pauline continued her narration before the choking fit had passed completely.

"It seems that the woman—this Olga Kaupiko—fell madly in love with one of her husband's kahus. Apparently the man returned her interest in him, and they became lovers."

Pauline coughed rigorously, but since the impulse was somewhat voluntary the fit was short-lived. Thoughts, like unexpected gusts of the tradewinds, raced through her mind, in which she questioned her right to continue telling the story. She struggled within herself for a taut, silent moment.

Some remembrances were sacred. A large pall of tabu surrounded them. Hawaiians had grown loath, in the years following Captain Cook's arrival, to talk about themselves. Their beliefs and habits had evoked such a thundering of Calvinist censure during the nineteenth century that they came to repress speaking of anything which might serve to expose them to further malediction. Pauline's willed halting in the telling of her story was automatically effected, for in training, and, to a large degree in spirit, she was very much a product of the nineteenth century.

Phillip, although a part-Hawaiian, was a product of haole education. He belonged to the present—to the confusing present—in which the old beliefs and the ancestral language were not passed on to the young.

Pauline struggled against the forceful impulse she had to tell him the story unsparingly, with all the details, as it had been told to her when she was a girl of eighteen. Frequently she questioned her propensity to remember certain things from the past which had a strongly biological connotation. Like this story. It led up to the inevitable end of so many stories Pauline recalled; and *why* were her memories so colored with incidents bearing, to one degree or another, upon the odium of human sexuality?

But since she couldn't bear to question herself beyond a certain point regarding this quaintly human preoccupation, she never carried her attempts at inward-directed analysis beyond a certain point.

This had spared her long hours of tortured self-abnegation; and it freed her, in the bargain, to continue recalling events from the past, hinged largely upon the thwarting or fulfillment of one biological function or another. She told stories of people being denied the privilege of urinating in certain bathrooms of the old aristocracy because they did not belong to the chiefly clan. Once she revealed to Phillip the incredible speculation that, since it was so cold in Moscow, she wondered if urinating out-of-doors, in the dead of winter there, caused the immediate forming of icicles. No dog was known to stray into her yard to accommodate itself without arousing one of Pauline's verbal explosions of disgust.

"I am really ashamed to tell you this story, Phillip. It is so revealing of one side of the character of our people. The sexy side."

Phillip Carysfort kept a serious countenance.

"You must admit that we really have that side!" Pauline continued, determined now to goad a commitment on the subject from her young visitor, sensing that the stern implacable expression he wore was censorious. Failing in this thrust, she went on, "Well, you don't know the old folks as I knew them!" There was a taunting inflection in her voice. "They were taken, hook, line, and sinker, with the subject. All their talk was simply crawling with references to the more carnal side of men and women!"

"What about Olga Kaupiko?" Phillip said, running his pencil idly over the page of his now-ready notebook. "We have wandered from the story of Olga."

"Well, my dear, you must give me time to warm up. You realize, of course, that I don't make a habit of telling these stories to everybody."

A loud wave of laughter, like the crashing of a foam-whitened breaker, filled the night's silence with another reminder of the raucous gaiety that filled the four tiny rooms of old Maka's cottage.

"Listen to that!" With sudden savagery, Pauline lifted one arm from her chair and aimed in in the direction of the cottage. "I am sure somebody is going to get raped tonight!"

"You were telling the story of Olga Kaupiko, Aunt Pauline!" the young man assailed, affecting the gesture of university classmates who were forever poised with notebook and pen during lectures of instructors who looked with favor upon such external manifests of scholastic avidity.

"O yes! Olga! Well," she paused:

"Those folks back there have been trying to get me to join them for the past three days—since the party began! I've flatly refused!" She willed herself to divert a while longer from the telling of Olga's story. "Old Maka has been quite drunk. This afternoon she came to ask me, for the twentieth time, to join them, and ended up by giving all the particulars of her love affair with old Ben. Imagine that! And she spared none of the details!"

With a seraphic coyness, Pauline turned her gaze away from the young man and sent a piercing look through the walls of her house to the neighboring cottage.

"Love dies hard among our old people," Phillip said consolingly.

"With some it lasts up to the last breath. Old Maka is seventy-five; and yet you should have heard her! The things she said, making motions and embellishing them with lewd sounds!"

"She merely wanted to share her amorous pleasures with you," Phillip teased gently.

"Indeed!" Pauline squawked like an alarmed hen, then chuckled softly, "It seems that her boy friend has a friend, who's been with them these past three days, whom old Maka has selected as a playmate for me! Imagine! He's a sergeant in the army! Such a thing to happen to me at my age! Besides, no one in our family has consorted with common soldiers!"

"These old people are so frank, so forward. Maka probably thinks she is doing you a big favor by making this sergeant available to you."

"They have no sense. I would tell the old thing to go packing, but what good would it do? It just doesn't occur to her that certain things just aren't mentioned in polite society. It means nothing to her to talk about extremely private matters, as you and I would discuss food or the weather."

Phillip Carysfort wondered if Pauline had any realization of the nature of her own conversational propensities. She could never fail to shock him, even after his having been exposed to remarkable and profoundly penetrating seminars under Dr. Kardiner at Columbia; or maybe, it was only because they were related that she could cause him such twinges of shock.

"A boy friend for me, mind you! Me with my asthma! How insulting!"

"I should think you would take this as a compliment."

"A compliment! to be laid before the altar of lust, choking and wheezing with asthma. Please, Phillip, spare me this! I haven't known desire since that awful time, years ago. I nearly died choking!"

There was no sadness or regret in Pauline's voice, much as she wanted to put across the image of a tragically helpless defloration.

It occurred unexpectedly to Phillip that this was the enigma of Pauline Irwin and others of their people. The restraints of education and religious training, hopelessly mingled with primordial archtypes of behavior, made it possible for Pauline to suffer indignation at one moment over the appearance of something that suggested licentiousness—such as Maka's three day charivari—and, at the very next moment, to be guilelessly frank about one's personal encounters with lust.

"I said to myself that I would never, never submit again. Of course it was really only a kind of experiment with me, that time long ago."

"Who was the lucky fellow, Aunt Pauline?" Phillip asked bluntly, the walls of his own restraint having crumbled under the weight of Pauline's intimate revelation.

"Kuli-kuli, be quiet, Phillip! There are some things you don't ask an old woman!"

"Sorry," he said with mock contrition.

"If you must know," she hastened on before he could lose interest, "it was a big Chinese-Hawaiian fellow. He had muscles on him like the bulges of a bag of sweet potatoes!"

"Love died with the one consummation?"

"Absolutely! He came round, time and again. I was living with Aunty Kanani then, out on King Street; but I told him to go seek some other flower on which to bestow his charms. I had a hell of a time convincing him that asthma and moe kolohe, mischievous sleeping, didn't mix.

"I certainly didn't want to die with that big bag of sweet potatoes on top of me!"

Her use of the post-missionary term of the Hawaiian for human mating charmed Phillip. Recently he had learned that it had come into being after 1820; that before then there would have been no occasion in Hawaiian life for it. Pre-European Hawaiians had looked upon certain things as mischievous, but never sex.

The vast walls, the socially constructed barriers against speaking or thinking of such things, fell after Pauline's intimate revelation and the force of their ensuing laughter mingled easily with the sounds issuing from the cottage on the other side of Pauline's high board fence.

"Did Olga Kaupiko have a similar fate as yours?" Phillip asked when he had stopped laughing.

"O, that damned Olga business. You simply won't forget it, will you?"

"I'm afraid you have made the first part of the story too tempting."

"Well," she sighed grandly, "Olga's kane manuahi, her boy friend, was put away by her kane male, her husband. He was poisoned, I think," She gestured carelessly. "Well, the old thing—I mean, Olga—was so lustful of this man that she had his private parts cut off, preserved them somehow, and kept them in a little silken sack. Ever after, she slept with her treasure under her pillow. Disgusting! Isn't it?"

"Not entirely. Some people take these matters very seriously. One sort of admires Olga's tenacious devotion to the memory of her lover. It was certainly a unique way of showing it. Beautifully primitive! And when she died? What happened to her keepsakes?" Phillip urged, relentless now to know all the facts.

"She mustered her strength, when she knew her time had come. She had her mementos divided into two parts and asked that they be planted under the two young sprouted coconuts growing outside her window."

"Gracious! What a touching tribute to the pleasures she had been granted."

"Hila-hila male! for shame!" Pauline said almost fiercely.

"Shame of what?" said a rasping voice outside the lattices of Pauline's back porch.

The statement was made in Hawaiian. Then in the lingua franca pidgin of the islands:

"What for shame! Nobody need be shame of notting!"

"It's that old wretch from behind," Pauline said in a half-jocular tone, forcing a slight smile to show on her face.

As much as she seemed to disapprove of some of old Maka's habits, she always viewed her as a quaint humorous relic growing miraculously from out of the deep marshes of the past.

"Come my house, no need be shame! Paulina, you everytime shame! 'Smatta wit you?"

Old Maka appeared in full sight in the doorway, bearing the marks in deshabille and reddened eyes of her three-day debauch.

"Hello, boy. How you?" she said to Phillip roguishly.

By his look, Phillip appeared to admire her mannish terseness.

Disregarding the proffered amenity, Pauline asked the old woman sharply when she and her guests were planning to end their celebration.

With a sweep of her right arm, as though she hoped to brush away, once and for all, every restriction that was ever put upon the continual pursuit of pleasure, the gaunt old woman said in a voice now strangely deepened:

"Nevah say die! Nevah say die! We can go on two-tree day moah!" then:

"I want you come ovah my house little while. You, Pilipo, you bring Paulina my house. We have a *good* time. We got plenny kau-kau an we got beah an wine." Her voice was honeysweet and remarkably youthful now.

"I only drink gin," Pauline said testily.

"Okay, I get geen too. One fella bring full *beeg* boddle," old Maka pressed on.

Phillip studied Pauline's face closely. He thought her cloaked smile revealed her desire to accept the invitation.

Again he thought of paradoxes. Given another cultural *milieu* and this would not have taken place. Pauline would have been settled in the comfortable interstices of Victorian spinsterhood. There would have been no old Maka temptress; there would have been no smile, denoting capitulation to the insistent offerings of hospitality. And, alas, there would have been no telling of the tale of Olga Kaupiko's treasure! Or, in another culture, it would have been madness.

"It wouldn't hurt for us to go over for a little bit, would it? Unless you have some place to go?" Pauline Irwin asked Phillip Carysfort plaintively.

Phillip shook his head.

"No, I'll be glad to take you over."

"You wait, Paulina, till you see the handsome soldier I've got over there for you. He's a sahgent! You're going to feel like a sweet little flower again, just waiting to be plucked," the old woman said in Hawaiian, adding with a sweetened smile, "You have wasted those beautiful hips and legs all these years. You ought to be ashamed of yourself. He mea mina-mina ia ka wahini ui—A beautiful woman is to be prized."

"I will never be able to impress on this old woman that my asthma positively rules out the possibility of my engaging in some of the cruder pleasures of life. I leave such things to this harridan and to the Olga Kaupikos of the world. Disgusting! Sometimes I think the good Lord showered a blessing upon me when he afflicted me with asthma."

She made a slight groaning sound to lend emphasis to the declaration.

"Now, let's go and see what all the racket is about back there." Her face was aglow with anticipation. Phillip took her arm and they followed old Maka out of the back door.

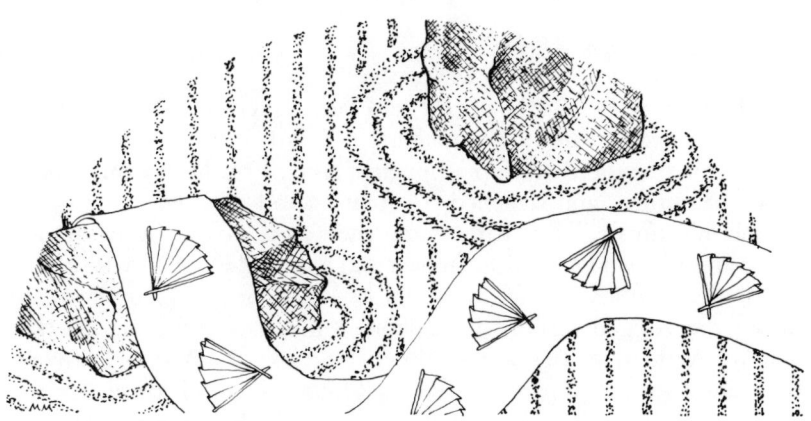

The Ditchman's Bride

For several days before we were to go to the ditchman Satoru Moriyama's house at Puukapu, Uncle Fred had told me about the marvelous country we were to ride through, how cold it was there on the slopes of the Kohala Mountains, and what a wonderful cook Moriyama was. Food being of great importance to a sixteen-year-old of my hedonist inclinations, the mention of fine cooking made me anticipate the visit to the ditchman at Puukapu with increased pleasure.

Daily at the absurd hour of four in the morning, Uncle Fred started off on his duties as a wandering trouble-shooting cowboy, hired in this capacity by a great ranch on the island of Hawaii because of his advancing years and because of his father's former connection with the ranch as an independent horse breeder. On the day we went to the ditchman's house at Puukapu, we left Uncle Fred's rambling old-fashioned house on the outskirts of Kamuela town an hour earlier than the usual incongruous hour he began his duties. The Puukapu paddocks were a long way from Kamuela—most of a day's ride, if you did not linger along the way.

Two cowboys, Ernest Moluhi and Joe Correa, who were to make another attempt to get at the renegade longhorn bulls wreaking havoc on the ranch's program to produce a pure strain of Herefords, were to join us in the trek to Puukapu.

Moluhi met us a mile or two down the road. He was a heavy-set young Hawaiian with a brooding, melancholy look. While Uncle Fred and Moluhi chattered away in Hawaiian, no doubt reviewing past attempts to rid the ranch of the lingering mongrel stock that still hid out in the heavily forested lands, I recalled the circumstances that involved my coming to visit Uncle Fred.

My father had strongly urged me to go to the Big Island to visit his cousin at the great ranch, once I had been asked.

We had been a family of ranchers. My father suffered a continual anxiety that I would end up a hopeless sissy. I read too many books, liked paintings, and listened to that "God-damned complicated symphonic music." Even if our ranches were gone, the lands now covered with rich fields of sugarcane and pineapple, the Newtons were essentially cowboys, as far as my father was concerned: cowboys still riding the rugged terrain of Makaha Valley, or galloping on their famous Arabian horses across the rich grassy plains of Halemano. Books and music and paintings were all right for "God-damned school teachers and the like," but not for a young Newton—especially one who was built on the same robust lines of the Newtons of the ranching days. He felt so strongly about this he had threatened once to break all of my phonograph records and to disown me if I spent another Saturday morning looking at Chinese and Japanese paintings at the Honolulu Academy of Arts. But I was enough of a Newton to love the out-of-doors as much as I loved music, books, and paintings so it had been no great sacrifice for me to accept Uncle Fred's invitation to spend the summer with him on the Big Island.

We rode the "soft shoulder" of the highway north for several miles before turning off to a dirt road lined with towering gum trees that led deceptively into the wilderness of finely grassed paddocks and the dark moist forest of koa and lehua trees. At the end of the eucalyptus-shaded roadway we met Joe Correa, a large, dark man, a part-Hawaiian, with eyes that seemed to penetrate the most secret reaches of your soul.

It was late afternoon by the time we emerged from a heavily-wooded ravine, thick with tree fern and lehua, lost somewhat under a fog now, to come upon a little knoll in an area well cleared of the luxuriant wilderness. In the center of the knoll sat the diminutive house of Satoru Moriyama. It was at once surrounded by a strange charm, a dream-like aura, conjuring for me poetic images of a Debussyian character. Snatches of *L'apres Midi d'un Faun* and *The Engulfed Cathedral* sounded in my ears, varied with bucolic reedy sounds and the atonal pluckings of the *koto* and *samisen*.

The house was a plain oblong affair of wood construction, gracefully embellished with touches of Japanese architecture: peaked roof, curving points where the roof joints met, and shoji doors. An arched cement bridge led over a clear water au'wai, a brooklet, that wound its way in a graceful path from the side of the house to collect in a large pool at the front. The pool was inhabited by a school of fat, slow-moving carp, colored brilliant orange, white, and black with here and there a mottled stray. Clipped shrubs had been planted in tasteful relation to groupings of rock—some naturally located, others arranged to simulate a natural appearance—a microcosm of the surrounding landscape. Over the entrance to the house grew a coniferous-type tree—probably a juniper—that had been forced by the wind to have an artistic lean in one direction. Its main trunk and larger branches were covered with a variety of mosses and lichens which created a superb patina of springy textures and muted color on the surfaces of bark—a fitting note to the entrance of the house, set as it was in so fine a garden.

"Ho! Moriyama-san!" Uncle Fred shouted. His roguish greeting was echoed by the two cowboys who rode up from behind.

I could not speak my thoughts. Uncle Fred, like my father, was not friendly to rhapsodic effusions over a beautiful sight, especially if they came from a male member of the family. He was all leather and muscle, with a mind and spirit molded by the dangerous rigors of the life of a Hawaiian cowboy of the old school. In the years spent chasing stray cattle and sheep over the cruel sharp deposits of a-a lava on the slopes of Mauna Kea, living on pai ai or half-dried taro paste, pipikaula or beef jerky, and hard tack, there had been no crevice open in his life for refining intellect or emotion in the aesthetic context.

While I let sensations of extreme admiration over the clean, sturdy grace of the little house and its surrounding garden possess me, I could see that Uncle Fred had already begun to feel a mounting sense of pleasure and anticipation. His face had arranged itself into contours expressive of bacchant exhilaration. He was ready and willing to revel in whatever delights were ahead, lying with magical pleasure-giving potentialities, in the food and drink that were to be offered us. Moriyama had known for two weeks of the impending visit, and he would have spared no effort in making preparations if all Uncle Fred had said about Moriyama as a host were true.

"Haddo, hello, Andrew-san!" A little figure in starched blue denim trousers and jacket appeared from one side of the house.

"Hai, hai, Moriyama-san!"

"Mai, mai, come, come," the little man said in Hawaiian in a husky voice. "I make hoch watta—suppose you dike take baht!"

The air was rich with the smell of burning wood and charcoal. These odors mingled effectively with smells of the surrounding woodland. It was a pungent sweetness, the mixture of decaying vegetation and the perfumes of various flowers whose scents escape from their imprisonment in pistils and stamens only after the sun has disappeared to brighten and warm another part of the world.

Uncle Fred had dismounted as gracefully as his years allowed, and asked Joe Correa to take care of his horse. Moriyama approached us, smiling. He seemed to be in a genuinely hospitable state.

"God damn, but the air is good up here," Uncle Fred declared, taking in deep breaths as he stood surveying the splendid little garden.

"Ass da bess kine aye-yah you can breat!" Joe Correa asserted, lingering on the scene, still mounted. "Ass da pure aye-yah from da mountin!"

Moluhi had silently and deftly managed to unload the pack horses and smiled a grateful response to my effort to help. As I helped Moluhi, I divided my attention between unsaddling the horses and keeping my eyes peeled to the entrance of Moriyama's house. Moluhi handed me bags and containers that held a food supply to last a couple of days. Among the parcels were presents of food from Uncle Fred and a special gift, a Hawaiian quilt—an heirloom—for the ditchman's bride. He had brought homemade sausage, a smoked turkey, two pheasants, and strips of salted pork. Uncle Fred was famous in the region for his skill in preserving and smoking the products of the land. His father had built a brick smokehouse in the opulent years of horse breeding. Though now in a state of near dilapidation, it was still usable.

"Come insigh, Ahndroo-san!" Moriyama said cheerfully

"You want to see me boil in that hot water riggin' of yours, I know!" Uncle Fred answered with his usual bluster.

"Leela bitch dreenko, kau kau first, moah betta. Bime bye insigh hoch watta! Now dreenko!" Moriyama himself was already flushed with drink. He led my uncle to the front stoop and detained him under the leaning stylish conifer.

"God-damned tree!" Uncle Fred blurted. "If it don't look like somebody chewed the hell outa one side of it!"

"Ass da way dey like um grow, Frad. 'Smatta wit you, Frad? Ass Japan style for grow tree!" Joe hurriedly interceded.

"New wife stop, Moriyama?" Uncle Fred asked.

"Yea! New wife stop. Kimiko-san! Kimiko-san!" Moriyama called and followed this with a few sentences in Japanese.

Uncle Fred crouched on a stool at the stoop and laboriously unbooted himself. At his home in Waimea, this daily late-afternoon ritual was accomplished with numerous grunts and sighs and other more gustatory sounds, interspersed with oaths of a strongly scatological character. He restrained himself now, uttering only a few disgruntled statements aimed at his boots and at the spectacle of encroaching age.

After carrying parcels and bags to the front door, I went with

Moluhi to stable the horses while Uncle Fred shouted orders after us about being careful where we put his saddle and other tack and the spot we chose to tether his near-Thoroughbred horse, Boar.

It was a delicious evening and I elected to stay out-of-doors to watch night fall silently upon the little house and its exquisite garden which was surrounded by a high mortar-free stone wall. There was scarcely a corner that was not developed into a general pattern of landscaping in the classic Japanese tradition. The cool moistness of the region, the amplitude of water, and the humus-rich soil made it possible for Moriyama to surround himself with a landscape, in miniature, that provided almost a perfect illusion of the environment he had left years ago, when he had made the long journey over the North Pacific Ocean to work in the cane fields of Hawaii and eventually become the caretaker of the great ditch at Puukapu which carried water from the rain-drenched, heavily forested Kohala Mountains to the little town of Waimea.

I learned, in time, that Moriyama had lived alone in this spot for some years following the death of his first wife. During the long isolated stretches between visits to the town of Waimea and the infrequent calls that were paid him by other employees of the ranch, he had worked upon improving his house and garden. Now, for almost a year, he had been married to a rosy-cheeked young girl whose relatives in nearby Honokaa had been instrumental in bringing her from Japan to be his bride.

A burst of laughter shot out of the house like the quick sharp explosions of lighted firecrackers. I was sure that drinks had already been served. The laughter was carefree and pleasant.

Joe Correa had followed Uncle Fred into the house as soon as he had unsaddled and tethered his horse. Moluhi joined me in my scanning of the garden. He was a sturdily-built fellow with the great, dark, love-hungry eyes of his race.

"Funny kine place dis! Like pu iopana keia garden."

I was surprised that he had lapsed into Hawaiian as he addressed me, forgetting that in the far rural areas of the "outside islands", those islands other than Oahu, some of the young people still used among themselves, to a degree, the indigenous tongue.

"Yes, it is just like a garden in Japan," I answered. "It is very beautiful."

"Dis firs' time you come ovah heah?"

"Yes."

"Dis my t'ird time. Me, I no like dis place—nui loa kela akua—there are many ghosts here!"

I chuckled, and he quickly admonished, "Don't be so shoo-ah of yooself. Me, I know dis contry like a book. Keia aina kolohe." This is a mischievous place, he had said, and sent his dark eyes searching lustfully in the crannies of the garden.

"It is a very isolated place," I said. "A perfect place for ghosts and spirits to lurk."

"Das what I mean! Da devils like dis kine place," he said with a shudder, and looked at me imploringly. "Way-ah you goin' sleep tonight, boy?"

"Inside, on the floor, I suppose. Isn't that where Japanese people sleep—on the floor?"

"I sleep nex' you, tonight. I no sleep by myself foah notting, dis kine place! Tomorrow I go out, try get da pipi laho hiuhiu, the wild bulls. I gotta have good sleep tonight."

Eat and drink were offered and taken plentifully, the repast served daintily by Kimiko on a low, round table at which we sat with our legs crossed. Uncle Fred had grown steadily more grandiosely gay and high-spirited as the evening progressed, playing drunken but restrained court to Kimiko who moved about with deft efficiency to serve us from the burning brazier and the rice pot. She kept a pan of chicken hekka cooking over the hibachi, never letting a plate sit empty for more than a few moments before she efficiently took it up and filled it once again with hekka and a scoop or two of rice.

"She's from the old school, this one," Uncle Fred said from time to time during the progress of the eating and drinking. "Very efficient and wifely! Very humble, as all women should be. You just can't beat these brides from Japan!"

I could see that Moriyama's pretty wife, with a demureness that was as delicate as fine lace, had captured Uncle Fred's fancy.

"Yes, indeed! A man could live like a king with so pretty and attentive a little flower running about to serve him," he said rapturously.

It was a strange, wonderful experience to be here in this little house in the wilderness of the Kohala Mountains, the guests of Mr. and Mrs. Satoru Moriyama, who were, in culture and language, so far removed from the familiar ruts of thought and living pattern which had fashioned me into the particular aggregate of custom, belief, and practice that I was.

Our home in Honolulu was situated in a crowded suburban corner, surrounded by houses of like style and size, with large rangy gardens around them, and telephones, radios, newspapers, automobiles, and crowds to fill each day with citified nuances. It was so vastly different from this doll's house.

Joe Correa had eaten and drunk with enormous dedication, as had the silent, fear-stricken Moluhi. Talk had been lavished upon the subject of their various activities in connection with the jobs they fulfilled as employees of the great ranch. They recalled epic round-ups of the past—Uncle Fred the only one who could boast of actual participation. Correa and Moluhi could only bask in the glory of their dead fathers' exploits.

There was talk of horses and stud bulls, famous in the annals of the ranch's history; of wild pigs that abounded everywhere on the ranch lands; of pheasant, of quail, and wild turkey. Joe Correa recalled his father telling him that once several thousand wild turkey had been gathered, as they roosted in the great koa trees on Mauna Kea's slopes, and sent to the markets in Honolulu. Uncle Fred told of famous old bulls that were tracked down and shot after years of freedom and hell-raising among the new herds of pure-bred Herefords.

He told also of losing a favorite dog which had fallen victim to the lashings of a great boar's tusks, and how, for more than thirty hours, he had waited for the angry beast to come out of a cave so he could lasso it from a perch above. When he had finally caught the huge pig in a noose of his kaula ili, he had used his horse to hoist the squealing brute into the air, just high enough for him to sink his hunting knife into the wild hog's belly. With a grim sense of triumph, Uncle Fred told of how he had stayed there and watched the pig dig into its own tormented belly with the sharp ivory tusks that had, a day or so before, inflicted deadly gashes upon the body of his favorite hunting dog.

Ranching people of Waimea were full of tales of encounters with wild pigs. They were a major nemesis of the more remote areas of the ranch. Moriyama, himself, had built the high stone wall surrounding his property as a means of keeping out the marauding black-coated wild pigs of the region.

Fortunately Kimiko Moriyama could not understand a word that was said, or she might have been shocked over and again at the talk that flowed ever more wildly as the night progressed.

Moluhi told of ghostly happenings in Waipio Valley, his place of birth. Uncle Fred chided him jocosely at first, and then more vehemently, as Moluhi continued to speak of seeing dogs and cats growing steadily to enormous size on the lonely dark trails of Waipio Valley. As you watched, a captive of the night and spirits, you were strangely thrown into a hypnotic state. Only if you were conscious enough to shout obscenities at the spirits could you make them disappear. If you managed to urinate, this also had the power to dispel.

Joseph Correa told of hearing ghostly processions pass by his cottage on the darkened nights of the moon, and how his Hawaiian grandmother had always advised him to lie flat on the floor and be very still when such things happened. Uncle Fred had declared the subject a bunch of crazy nonsense and flatly changed the subject by asking Moriyama to sing.

"You singo firs', boss! You singo!"

"Hell, man! I've got the worst voice in the whole of Waimea!" he shrieked and fell into a wild fit of coughing.

I knew he had brought along his ancient concertina upon which he played for hours on Saturday nights in Waimea when he got wholeheartedly drunk on okolehao, the native spirit, which someone always sent up to him in large five-gallon demijohns from Waipio Valley. When I reminded him that he had brought his concertina, and that Joe had thoughtfully carried it into the house after we arrived, he emerged from the coughing and called me a ni'ele or nosy little-son-of-a-bitch, at which point I went for the little instrument, removed it from its aged case, and brought it ceremoniously to him before anyone forgot that he had just been asked to sing.

Uncle Fred had grown alarmingly florid after the taking of so much food and drink. His skin, ordinarily pink and of excellent tone, seemed now to be taut and red as a radish. "But, never let it be known that Fred Andrews ever refused to be accommodating when he was asked to do something!" he said with a mock heroic air. "Singing, I come by quite naturally. Both my parents had beautiful singing voices!"

"Singo, Androo-san, singo!"

Moluhi leered at Uncle Fred with eyes now ominously reddened by too much drink. I began to see this strangely quiet man as a person of hidden malevolence. He said things under his breath in the Hawaiian tongue. I was sure they were scathing portentous oaths cast upon Uncle Fred's callous disinterest in Moluhi's occultist tendencies. But I discovered Moluhi's demoniac look to be an over-dramatization on my part: instead of leaping up and giving vent to a submerged wrath, the logical fulfillment of his facial expression, Moluhi rose from his place at the low table and went quietly to another part of the room to get his guitar. From somewhere, Joe Correa unearthed a ukulele.

The singing and the strumming of the stringed instruments, the baleful tones of Uncle Fred's concertina, and his attempts at making song, filled the night with a gaiety and spirit that these parts had perhaps never known. Moriyama sat and swayed his body with the rhythms of the music. His wife swiftly cleared the table of stove and dishes and eating utensils, and disappeared from view.

The Ditchman's Bride 83

"Now, it's your turn, Moriyama, your turn!"

"Kimiko-san! Kimiko-san!" Moriyama called several times, but there was no answer.

In compliance with his unanswered call, I went to the little kitchen, and then outside to a connecting woodshed. Here, I heard distinctly the piteous sobbings of a child. The sobbing was soft and gracefully mournful, like the cry of certain birds who loiter and feed along lonely marshy stretches of beach. It was Kimiko who was sobbing. Her embarrassment was unbounded when she saw that I had been standing nearby for a few moments, watching her cry. I pointed to the inside of the house. Moriyama once again called for her.

Kimiko was ordered to get out a koto, one of the stringed instruments of old Japan, to accompany her husband in his singing effort. We sent up a rousing applause and waited. Here was Cho-cho-san of *Madame Butterfly;* here had materialized the storied geisha who, for some reason, had never appeared in Hawaii in spite of our large Japanese population. She began to pluck the instrument slowly, almost with a caressive sort of gesture, giving Moriyama the chance to gain a rigidity in his back as he sat waiting for the moment to come for him to sing the first notes of his song.

Why had I found his bride of less than a year sobbing with such a depth of sadness only a few moments ago? Moriyama was strong and had excellent looks. That his spirit was tough, and he was in possession of himself, was certainly proved in his living with such devoted artistry for so many long years, alone in this detached corner of the Hawaiian Islands. That he was sensible, kindly and civilized, had been made clearly evident to me this evening as I had watched him perform the duties of a host with skill and inordinate generosity, from the moment of our arrival. It seemed strange that Kimiko should suffer discontent, living with such a man as her Satoru Moriyama.

He sang playfully but with restraint. Moriyama was not a professional singer; this he explained to us in a burst of self-defense with a flood of sucked-in and spat-out words. It was evident that Moriyama was very drunk. So far as the men were concerned, the evening had been a great success. I, myself, could not feel, in truth, that the talk or the singing—particularly the singing—had been of estimable quality. It was roughly hewn, like Uncle Fred, Joe Correa and Moluhi themselves were, in body and spirit. The strange words and the stranger manifests of emphasis and restraint in the half-spoken recitative type of song that the Moriyamas were performing gave to the night a peculiar quality of loneliness and exotica.

It brought to my mind the scenes depicted on the great screens, or panels, or scrolls, that were exhibited at the Academy of Arts in Honolulu, of birds and animals, flowers and trees, and houses in which people with massive and elaborate hair stylings, dressed in brocaded kimonos, sat, fought, or danced, or simply stared out at you in reflective monastic contemplation. "This is like old Japan," I whispered to Uncle Fred. "Like the scenes you see in the Kakemono scrolls, or the big screens."

"Bull shit!" he answered, rolling his steel-gray eyes. "This is Hawaii," he said, and dispelled any further need for pursuing the subject by giving way to a coughing fit.

I was used to his brusque outbursts. Indeed, they were somewhat like my father's; and having forgot that he was insensitive, even intolerant, of anything that was of a wistful, artistic quality, I felt that I deserved the terse and vulgar admonition. In truth, Uncle Fred may not have even known of the existence of the Honolulu Academy of Arts since he had made only two trips to our island during his lifetime: once as a youth, long before the museum had come into existence, and again when I had been invited to return with him to Waimea. As a cowboy of his generation, art museums were of little importance in his life.

It was to Kimiko that I directed my thoughts after this. Why had she taken herself to the woodshed to cry with such heartbreak, with such sobbing? Why had she come to Hawaii in the first place? Who had she been, and what had she done before coming to be Moriyama's bride? I enjoyed considering this and pondering it as a mystery. In my musings, I finally became aware of Joe Correa clapping wildly and asking for another song. His enthusiastic outbursts diverted my thoughts. Kimiko's head was bowed, and in Japanese Moriyama gave her instructions with a gruffness that I had not seen displayed in him before.

"Nudda song! Nudda song! Nudda song!" Joe intoned like a baying hound dog.

"Hana hou! Hana hou!" Moluhi grunted, repeating in Hawaiian Joe's request for another song.

It was all quite silly, even a little ridiculous; and with my knowledge of what had happened before Kimiko had come in to play and sing, there was already an element of pathos in the scene. If Kimiko were as sober as I, she would be as bored; or perhaps more than this, she could be incensed at the invasion of her husband's friends into the pristine order of her home.

But Moriyama was used to these invasions. According to Uncle Fred, he welcomed them. In the long years of his bachelorhood he had depended on sporadic debauches taking place when Uncle Fred and some of the ranch people descended upon him to enjoy his food and drink, and, although I believe they did not consciously realize this, to enjoy also the beauty of his little home. This was the second friendly "bender" to take place since Kimiko had joined her lot to Moriyama's. Obviously she was not as content and happily absorbed in the celebrating as her husband.

The revelling had held the promise of demise for some time before patent demonstration of human exhaustion and paralyzing drunkenness was displayed. Quite suddenly, Uncle Fred fell from a sitting position into a deep and snoring sleep. I had not expected the night's gaiety to come to such an ignominious conclusion. The mind of the young debauchee is ever hopeful that, no matter how dull and repetitive the product of merrymaking, it should be interminable.

With what seemed to me an unnecessary and noisy struggle we put my aging cousin to bed in a little room the ditchman had indicated with many gestures and much sputtering, as the place he had chosen for Uncle Fred and me to sleep.

"You waste time, Frad Androosh!" Joe spewed drunkenly. "You no can take eet. 'Smatta wit you, Frad! Da night ees young yat!"

The mutterings complicated our effort. Moluhi and the ditchman had joined me to maneuver my cousin's large and heavy body toward the little bedroom. From the depths of his intoxication Uncle Fred had boldly tried to answer Joe Correa's accusations, saying in unintelligible grunts and growls the foolish things that a drunken man will attempt to say in the effort to keep personal dignity and honor intact.

I asked Joe to stop taunting Uncle Fred. His attempts to answer the jibes began to complicate putting him to bed. Like a floundering, momentarily inept animal, his body swayed, and he flung his large heavy-boned arms in all directions. Joe stopped the teasing and began to sing a Portuguese love song.

Kimiko had in the meantime skittered about, arranging sleeping pads and silk-covered quilts to cover Uncle Fred's ponderous body the moment we were able to jimmy it into recumbency. Joe's song seemed a fitting musical accompaniment to our act of arranging Uncle Fred for his night's rest. There was pathos and resignation in the minor tones of the song; its melody was richly suggestive of the darkened huts of a Portuguese fishing village.

A note of desire had crept into Joe Correa's voice, like the tone in an animal's cry which distinguishes the mating call from the cry of alarm. It became evident to my sixteen-year-old's cognizance that Joe, too, had become filled with desire for the flower-like Kimiko.

After getting Uncle Fred settled, I went outside for a breath of air. The night was dark enough to allow the sky and its blinking planetary and celestial bodies to have the brilliance of diamonds. It was so quiet you could hear the smallest sounds that insects made. The air, still, and cleared now of its obfuscating and dampish fog, compelled me to take deep lungfilling breaths that made my whole body pulse with exhilaration. Being alive seemed to achieve a new significance. My adolescent wonder at cosmogonic mysteries, which usually shook me to the foundations of my soul—and which I was tempted to pursue at such moments as the present one—seemed of little consequence now. The night's beauty devoured me in the gnawing human element of curiosity and speculation. For a moment I felt as though a poem of Whitman's I had recently been exposed to in a literary appreciation class had been written especially for me.

Before going outside, I had noticed that Moluhi had found a spot in which to sleep in a corner of the main room of the little house. I was sure he would be safe from the haunting presences of Hawaiian ghosts. Joe Correa had gone to the back of the house to urinate, continuing his song so that it became a charming leit motif of the night's fabric. Moriyama had quietly gone to his room and passed out after we had successfully bedded down Uncle Fred for the night.

When I was certain that all was quiet for the night, that the four happily drunken men were safe in the throes of their slumbers, and that it would be time now for me to go in and make my own capitulation to the state of sleep, I heard Kimiko's faint cries of protest.

"No, no!" she said, interspersing this with short sentences in Japanese. "No, no!" she cried out in anguish. Even in this disturbed state, her tone of voice had kept its delicate quality.

I was not surprised to see that Joe Correa was the cause of Kimiko's distress. He held her tightly around the waist and was trying to kiss her.

"No, no!" she protested. "No, no!" she cried again and again, attempting to extract her dainty body from his massive arms.

"Joe!" I called. He answered a surly, *shut up!* adding stronger expletives to register his anger at my intrusion. I went to him, and he knocked me over with a quick blow of his right arm.

"Go insigh, you bugga, or I going geeve you good leeking!"

"You can't do this, Joe!" I said from my humiliating position on the ground.

"No can doh! No can doh! No can doh!" Kimiko chanted delicately, and freed herself from Joe's embrace after concentrating her small strength in a single exertion.

"Godama you, keed!" Joe said angrily. "I like dat leedle piece toonight, keed! 'Smatta, you com butt een?" He weaved on great legs that ordinarily gave him superb and unfaltering use.

"You can't do that, Joe! You'll get in trouble!" I said gasping, and rose from the ground. "You might do something you would be sorry about for the rest of your life!"

In a moment his great arms had encircled my body which he held rigid in a vise-like embrace. "You one Goddam good keed! You save Joe from planny trouble!" He lifted me from the ground and twirled unsteadily, pressing his sandpaper-bearded face against mine.

"Go to sleep, Joe!" I said, after squirming free of his tautly muscled arms. "Go to sleep, Joe! We have things to do in the morning."

"I got tings to do right now, keed. I gotta take a leek again! Right now!" he said in a deep gutteral tone, and fell in a heap to the ground.

It was one of the physical triumphs of my life to get Joe Correa into the house and settled into the spot that had been set up for him as a sleeping place. I tugged, cajoled, pleaded, and cursed for what seemed like a period of several hours, before I was finally able to spread a thick cotton-batting quilt over the paralyzed form of Joe Correa, and walk off, muttering embarrassing obscenities as a way of appeasing my outraged feelings.

"Goodnight!" I said in a stage whisper. "You filthy———drunks!"

There was not the slightest stir in the house when I finally fell upon my sleeping pad in the little room, reeking now with the liquor Uncle Fred had drunk and noisy with respiratory noises that gushed from his comatose frame.

It must have been three in the morning when I awoke, hearing again the faint childlike sobs of distress. Like the tinkling of fragile exotic bells, the sobbing added a delicate, incongruous note to the collective snoring of the four drunken men which had filled the little house with the reassuring noises of deep slumber when I had come to the room to bed down for the night.

Several minutes passed before I became aware that Kimiko had ceased crying. The tinkling contrapuntal embellishment to the men's snoring had been so audible that without it, that the atmosphere assumed a new character.

I was loath to throw off the cotton-stuffed quilt that had been provided me for the night, and go to investigate Kimiko's sobbing. It was cold. I thought of the blinking crystalline heavens, the dark forms of trees, roaming pigs, and Moluhi's ghosts, which only strengthened my determination to stay quietly under the engulfing quilt. Then, for some reason, my awareness that the crying had stopped became charged with curiosity or portent, or perhaps a combination of both. Quickly I threw off the quilt, rose silently, and left the room.

Carefully I picked my way across the room in which the two paniolos were asleep, to a place where three steps led down to a little room that was furnished with a single flat table, in the corner of which sat the gilded cabinet which served as an altar or shrine in many homes of the Japanese of those days when I was young.

A lantern, burning a low flame, sat on the table, the flickering reflection of its light lingering on the gilded metal fittings of the cabinet. Before it, bent over in a precisely-achieved foetal position, lay the form of Kimiko. One side of her face lay gently on the reed matting which covered the floor. Her black eyes were open, fixed in an accusing stare on one section of the wall. A pool of blood had begun to coagulate under her bent knees.

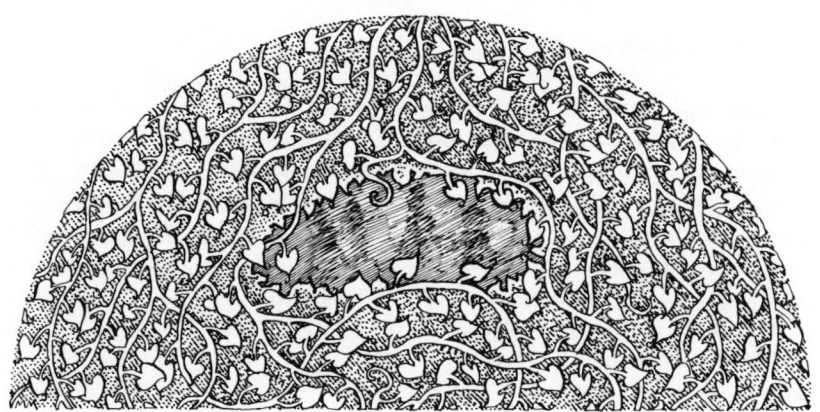

"So Long as a Man's Family Continued in Possession of a Cave"

"I had spotted it one day while idly studying the cliffs at Kahakuloa—an opening in the rocky descent. There, about halfway down, was the opening—a crevice that had been appropriated by a family of Boatswain birds. I was struck, for some mysterious reason, with the possibility of this small opening in the cliff being the entrance to a burial cave."

My old friend, Julian Carter, had come to New York from the islands of my birth with a manuscript telling of some of his experiences as an unofficial explorer of Hawaiian burial caves. Somehow this story which he began to tell had not been included in the contents of his manuscript. I urged him to tell the story when he had made a few more sketchy references to the Kahakuloa cave after we had retired to more comfortable sitting arrangements in the living room of our New York apartment.

"I went back the next day, and the day after, searching the plateau above the cliff for another entrance. There might well have been a more accessible entrance on the flat land above, but I could not find it. The Hawaiians were very clever in hiding the bones of their dead—especially the bones of royal or noble persons." Julian paused, reflecting intently before he continued telling of his adventure. He always kept the air of an instructor, a learned expert, when he discussed Hawaiiana, taking for granted that everything he had to say was new knowledge for the listener, no matter how much the listener himself might have known about the old way of life in Hawaii. "A curious thing had happened," he said. "Each day I encountered the same old man at the spot."

"You mean a ghost?" I interrupted facetiously.

"No," Julian answered courteously. He was devoted to his subject to the point of being impervious to light-hearted remarks. "No, he was just an old man—one of the people from the tiny settlement situated about a mile into the valley. It was one of those isolated, beautiful valleys that breathe an air of classic antiquity. The islands are dotted here and there with such unspoiled valleys. The Hawaiians find them and form last-ditch communities—the last strongholds of indigenous living, usually held together by one strong figure, the prototype reactionary clinging to a golden dream of the past, wanting nothing more than a reversal of time and circumstance." He paused and smiled.

"My wife's grandfather is such a person," he said in a cheerful, personal way. "You know the old man, old Pana-Ewa. He's always talking of his kahuna powers and predicting all sorts of disaster to befall the unbelieving—the infidel outsider like myself. After all, I'm only an intrusive haole, forever snooping into the secrets of the Hawaiian past. I suppose, if the truth were known, that is the only reason I married the old fellow's granddaughter. That, and of course, the old libido egging me on unwittingly."

"Mokihana has her attractions," I said, "as well as historic artifacts."

"A fortunate combination so far as I'm concerned. Mokihana is a living reminder. Trouble is, she grew resentful of my entering burial caves. Too much of her grandfather in her." Julian let his eyes sweep quickly down to the street below our windows to the now darkened mass of Central Park. "Understandable, I suppose," he said quietly and brought his gaze back into the room. "I have never told her about the Kahakuloa cave and my experience there, and I hope you won't be hu-hu after I've told you the complete story tonight." There was a trace of the Cheshire cat's grin on Julian's face. A sardonic gleam followed, not entirely in character with his usual demeanor.

"I'm sure I needn't be angry," I hurriedly assured him, and attempted to show no evidence of my having detected in his look a suggestion of sadistic delight. He was fully aware of the effect that talking about burial caves has on Hawaiian people.

"I had returned to the spot above the cliff the following day," he began again. "It was morning. I hoped to map plans for entering the cave. I had driven there in the little Dodge convertible that your cousin Mavis has always so kindly placed at my disposal during my archeological foragings on Maui. I had thought at first it would be difficult to find the spot again. It wasn't. I had no trouble locating it."

Julian had a keen eye for topographic details. On a number of occasions, when I had roamed with him certain valleys and coastal areas of Oahu, I had been naively impressed with his ability to spot landmarks and relate them immediately to a location of specific importance. If we came upon idyllic mountain pools, or a growth of endemic and rare Hawaiian flora, or the vestiges of an ancient rock-walled heiau, he would scan the surrounding area, choose easily identifiable objects within the region as a means of preserving the locality of our discovery and say triumphantly, "Remember those trees, or those rocks over there. They will serve you as markers if you ever want to come back." And I would have futilely scanned the area, searching for landmarks that had made themselves so clearly apparent to Julian, but which somehow had eluded me.

"I had marked the location of the cave by remembering two—oddly enough, only two—coconut palms growing some distance away which seemed to have been planted with the intent of their serving as landmarks. That was done, you know, in the old days. Hawaiians planted trees to preserve identification of burial places or the location of something else of prized value. They were so secretive in these matters. They had to be. There were strong beliefs concerning the harm that could be inflicted upon departed souls should the physical remains of persons fall into the hands of vengeful enemies. You see, life wasn't all the idyllic pleasure-filled dream which scenario writers and novelists love to portray in their stories of Polynesia. There was colossal fear and anxiety in many areas of the average Polynesian's life. But they developed a means to cope with these. They did not live in confusion, or the fear that comes from extreme want, or an emptiness of the soul." He spoke the final statement with an air of indignation and authority which some students of exotic cultures adopt in their fervent desire to countermand the castigating and irresponsible opinions of nineteenth-century missionaries who so faithfully recorded their impressions of stone-age Pacific island cultures as they settled into them to spread the message of Christianity.

"To get back to my cave," Julian said, annoyed at his self-propelled flight away from the subject. "I had no sooner arrived and left the car when I saw him again—the old man. The same old fellow I had seen the day before. He was sitting on a rock, quietly. He seemed so self-contained—dressed in black serge trousers. You know the kind of trousers that Hawaiians of another generation so loved to wear." Amused with his summoning of the sentimental image of Hawaiian men in narrow black serge trousers, Julian's eyes twinkled with a child-like innocence. It was an ingrained characteristic of his behavior to smile this way when he spoke of some of the manifests of the human spectacle. "The old man also wore a white shirt—a regular dress shirt, open at the collar. No tie. He seemed so properly attired for the occasion—a figure out of the nineteenth century." Julian chuckled lovingly, a shortish appreciative chuckle which caused him to smile again, this time more broadly. "It was one of those little sights you meet up with in fringe communities of the Hawaiians that make you sad, and yet are pleasing in their almost classic simplicity.

"The old man stared at me—a peculiar stare that had an almost trancelike aspect. It was not one of hostility—nor was it one of curiosity. It had a strangely timeless character—like the look you see in the countenances of sculptured figures of the Greco-Roman and Buddhist worlds. It was really a haunting look, and somehow it did not belong to the present.

"I made an effort to speak. I said a crude pehea oe—you know how stilted my Hawaiian is—and I smiled. Without returning the greeting, the old man turned away and impulsively left the spot, taking a path which seemed obviously to lead to the village down below. I tried to keep him in sight, but soon his figure—now wraithlike, the misty outlines of something in motion—disappeared into the thickets of lantana and guava."

"Well, who was he? Did you make an effort to find out? You have already denied that he was a ghost."

My friend only smiled—a smile that contained all the ephemeral vagary of his own description of the look of the old man he had encountered above the cliffs of Kahakuloa. He did not answer me. Instead, he continued:

"This opening I had spotted in the cliff was difficult to reach, making the cave, into which it might lead, the more valuable as a repository for the dead. The more inaccessible a cave, or the more carefully hidden its orifices, the more important were the people who were likely to be buried there."

I felt at this point like reminding Julian that I was reasonably acquainted with some of the ways of my aboriginal predecessors and that the secrecy involved in burying the great chiefs of the past was something that had been drummed into me from childhood. The fact that Kamehameha the Great's burial place has never been discovered is common knowledge to all islanders, let alone Hawaiians.

"The chiefs were beset with enemies—malcontent relatives, rival chiefs, and the like," he continued in the sonorous tones of the born pedagogue. "In the old beliefs, a person's spirit or uhane could be maligned if objects having any relationship to the deceased were prayed over by the sorcery-ridden kahunas."

Then his face lighted up, and he said almost with a sense of triumph, "In the days after contact with sea captains and merchants and money, valuables—in our sense—were introduced and accumulated by the chiefs, so some of them were buried with considerable treasure. This created another incentive for secrecy in choosing burial caves. It was at this time that some chiefly families had the remains of their ancestors transferred to even more remote and inaccessible places. Now they had to contend with treasure seekers. In one age the incentive for robbing a cave was spiritual, and in another age it became profit!"

"You keep thinking that you are addressing a meeting of naive old ladies, or a group of freshmen being introduced to some highly subjective evaluations of an amateur sociologist," I said with some irritation, for even if the years in New York had separated me from my home and its antiquities for some time now, I had not forgot what I had heard or read about ancient Hawaiian burial practices.

"I'm sorry," Julian said with a wounded look. "I keep forgetting how well-informed you are in Hawaiian lore. So many people aren't. Especially here in a place like New York."

"Of course you are somewhat an expert, and the urge to teach burns away within you," I said as a means of assuagement.

Julian's smile of innocence again possessed the contours of his face. "I'll try to resist the impulse to instruct, if you want me to go ahead with the story of my adventure at Kahakuloa," he said with a dignified tone.

Allowing a comforting interval of silence to elapse, Julian again took up the threads of his story:

"But it was after I had seen the old man loitering in the area of the opening in the cliff for the third time that I decided to try to enter it at night." And here he paused again as though waiting for some muse to fire his thoughts with another surge of brilliant imagery.

"I never dreamed Kahakuloa would have anything of archeological value," I said perfunctorily. "It has always seemed so desolated, so uninviting, as though in any age no humans would choose to live there."

"That's just it. It was a place of importance in the early times—a great place for burials. The cliffs dictated this."

"It's hard to imagine," I said flatly. "One of my calabash uncles had a small slaughter house and dairy out there. I was about twelve when I first visited Kahakuloa. It seemed like the very end of the earth—so quiet and isolated—so undistinguished, really."

"That's perhaps its character in the present day. In another time it might have flourished as a community." Julian smiled, registering patience with my unscientific views. "As I said," he continued, "I planned to return to the spot that night."

Vestiges of the distant past which lingered in the vast territory of my psyche rankled as he made the last statement. In spite of a considerable thinning of the aboriginal blood through the intervention of generations of time and the modern American education I had acquired which, by and large, spoofs at any belief in the occult, I chilled at the thought of Julian daring to enter the sacred precincts of a burial cave in daylight—let alone, in the dark of night. "You went to the cave at night?" I demanded with an almost vulgar intensity.

"I certainly did. That very night. A marvelous night for my intentions. It was in the wane of the moon—very dark and very still. After seeing the old man for the third time, I suspected that he was the surviving kahu, the caretaker, of the tomb, and he had become chary after seeing me there twice before. I was forced to go back at night if I wanted even to explore the possibility that the opening in the cliff led to a burial cave. Going on the supposition that most Hawaiians are fearful of the night, I assumed he wouldn't be there after dark; and that, if I used a small flashlight not visible from the village, my chances of entering the cave undetected were very good."

"Didn't you have any qualms? Most people would have been fearful enough to enter such a place in daylight, let alone, in the darkness," I said, bringing my thoughts of a few moments ago into the realm of the spoken word.

"I have learned not to be taken in by the nonsense people speak in relation to Hawaiian burial caves—ghostly reprisals and the like. I couldn't be fearful and continue to explore these caves. Besides, there is something about the occult that is positively insulting to a grown-up human intelligence."

"But you have such a respect, such a warm feeling for Hawaiian culture. I should think you might easily have been influenced by the talk of supernatural elements in Hawaiian lore. The burial caves are of particular sacerdotal importance, and, as such, they are surrounded by billowing clouds of the occult," I argued.

"Such matters affect certain people in certain ways. Superstitions seem almost to be bred into Hawaiians. But I have never been concerned much with supernatural essences, one way or the other. They do not interest or scare me."

At this moment I was filled with the insight that I had never really known Julian Carter. We had been friends for many years, rather intimate friends, and yet I had never seen this ruthlessly objective side of his personality. Or, was it because superstitions had been "bred into" me and not Julian—the knowledge of this suddenly creating him a stranger. Julian, having no awareness of my speculations, proceeded with his story:

"I returned to the cliff that night. I had bought a small flashlight, some candles, a poleman's climbing belt, and about a hundred feet of heavy-grade rope. I drove to the spot in the early evening and parked Mavis's roadster about a hundred feet from the opening in the cliffside. I took every precaution to make sure I was not observable from the village." He smiled, caught again in the net of romance which he felt about so many things Hawaiian. "There it was in the distance—the little village—each house softly lighted up. My heart ached for a moment. I've always been moved at the sight of these 'last-ditch' Hawaiian communities that cling to an existence closer to the ancient times in character, removed from other people in pathetic and determined isolation. You still find these communities in Kona; in fact, all over the Big Island. You also find them on Kauai. Even on Oahu, with the vast encroachment of Honolulu upon anything like these ethnocentric nuclei, there are still a few—such as Waikane with its staid little church."

"I should think that these feelings of sympathy and nostalgia would have caused you to give up your furtive, your stealthy, expedition," I interrupted under another stimulus of irritation.

"Why so?"

"Well, if you felt so much aloha for these Hawaiians in the valley at Kahakuloa, you would have hesitated doing anything that might upset or anger them. At this point the old man was apparently aware of your designs on the cave, and in preparing to return to the place, you took precautions not to be seen by him, or any of the villagers—knowing damned well it would arouse them in some way."

"You are right, but you are presuming that I was about to do a criminal thing."

"Weren't you?"

"No. If I were an idle treasure seeker—a thief—yes."

"Your interests, being purely scientific, removed you automatically from the odium of being a grave robber?"

"In a way, yes."

"I must say, that aside from admiring your fearlessness, I congratulate you on your ability to rationalize your way so deftly out of an immoral position."

"I don't think that's quite fair. I do collect—unofficially of course— for museums and for people with well-established and representative collections. I have never once *felt* like a thief or a despoiler, or a sacrilegious flesh-pot in exploring Hawaiian burial caves. I have never once disturbed the remains of people, nor have I ever left a cave in a disordered state. I only take that which I think may be of scientific interest to the museums and reputable collectors."

"How far we have wandered from your tale. I apologize if I've cast a shadow of doubt on your motives," I said.

Julian rose, made a quick sortie about the room, doubling back to avoid my wife Helen's lazy, fat, black cat which obstructed his passage near the fireplace. Having managed to release any build-up of annoyance, he sat down again, in a matter of seconds, and continued his story:

"The long and short of matters is that I did maneuver myself to the opening in the cliff and I did enter the cave." He said this with uncharacteristic emphasis.

"Was it a beauty?" My question popped out with the same immediacy with which a room becomes illuminated when an electric switch is turned on.

"It was indeed a beauty—the most beautiful burial cave I have ever seen." Then his eyes sparkled with excitement, and his voice took on a somber, reverent tone. "It was large—from what I could see after I lighted the candles—and simply crammed with stuff. A canoe, tapa cloth in heaps everywhere, sea chests, clothing, kahili standards, surfboards, numerous stone and wood objects—even books. It was, quite apparently, the burial place of an important Maui family."

My spirit froze. I envisioned a vaporous oozing of mist, then monosyllabic chanting, and finally some act of mystic retaliation.

"It was a marvelous discovery. Certainly the largest and most lavish burial collection I had ever seen. I had begun to search quickly for a feather cloak or feather capes—often these were buried with the alii. A number of capes have been found in burial caves. None were immediately apparent." Then he stopped, said nothing for a few moments before continuing: "There must have been thirty or forty people buried there. And some of the coffins were quite new!"

"New *coffins?*" I asked incredulously.

"Yes. Apparently the family who used this as a burial cave had continued to use it into modern times. I had never encountered this before. I must admit that I began to chill a bit at this point, but I was fascinated. Here were ancient artifacts and clothing, and here in another section were coffins and books, even pictures—a couple of paintings, daguerreotypes, and more recent photographs. I searched frantically for some featherwork objects—they have the most value and are extremely scarce. Wood carvings of the old deities are also rare, and I thought I saw several in the cave that night, but I was so intent on finding a feather cape, I overlooked the carved wood objects.

"Suddenly I was beset with premonitions. I thought I heard

drumbeats and chanting. Strange gusts of air flowed through the cave, freshening and cooling it marvelously. Then I thought I heard voices in the distance. Real and alive human voices. I quickly gathered up some tapa cloth and stuffed it into my poleman's climbing belt. I grabbed for some trinkets—shell and dogtooth necklaces and bracelets. I don't really know why, but I reached for a couple of the books and made quickly for the opening in the cliff. I put out the candles and used the small flashlight."

"You must have been in quite a state at this point, a little torn between running and staying to harvest," I said with a weak laugh, attempting to dispel the sense of fear that swept through me. "But what I can't get over is your having seen books among the objects in the cave."

"I was in such a state I dropped one of the books into the sea below, and would have lost the trinkets if I hadn't stuffed them into my trouser pockets. I had a hell of a time scaling that cliff—it involved about forty feet of climbing. I had stuffed the book into my shirt before starting the climb and it poked into my ribs. But I ignored the irritation and kept climbing to the top. I had anchored the rope onto a tough guava tree stump and had no fear that it wouldn't hold. When I reached the top of the cliff and landed flat on my stomach, nearly gored by the guava stump, the fun really began."

"You had been seen."

"Exactly, and in the distance I could see kerosene lanterns swinging in the darkness, and I could hear the voices of men shouting angrily. At this point I was really worried. I had left three hundred dollars in the car. I had carefully stashed the bills—fives, tens, twenties, and a number of one dollar bills—under one of the pads which protected the canvas from the framework of convertible roadster tops in those days. I made a run for the car, dumped my gear and findings in the back seat, and reached for the money. I don't know how I had the wits to make sure of my money, but I did."

"You're not going to tell me now that it was gone?"

"Precisely. It was gone. It had been scattered all around the car. I discovered this soon enough after flashing light on the ground—an instinctive reaction. I frantically gathered up as much of the money as I could find, eventually collecting a little more than two hundred dollars. I stopped searching when I saw the lanterns approaching closer and at a faster rate. When I attempted to start the car, the damned thing choked a couple of times and had to be started again. It was terrifying—like something out of an African adventure story, natives running down the white intruder, and all that." Julian chuckled with choked-up intensity evident in the good-humored sound.

"Believe me, I felt weird." He was not smiling now. "I drove away from that cursed spot with a sense of utter relief—and you have no idea how comforting automobile headlights can be in a situation like that one. In a matter of a few minutes I had left the whole scene behind and dared to stop to look back after driving for a mile or so. The lanterns were clustered in a group—perhaps six of them—and I could only imagine the angry shouts of the men who had come after me."

"How do you explain the money being taken from your car—from its hiding place—and spread over the surrounding area?"

"I have no explanation for that."

"Do you suppose the old kahu had been watching you all the time and had removed the money and strewn it about as a means of detaining you when you had come back from exploring the cave? Hawaiians are so indifferent to money, and they know how much haoles worship it," I said with petulance, growing impatient with my own kind after accepting my thesis as the truth.

"I don't know. I haven't even a theory. Perhaps your guess is as good as any. Probably that's the reason I omitted this story from the collection in my book. But I still have one of the objects I brought out of the burial cave that night. As a matter-of-fact, I brought it with me to New York. It's in one of my bags now. I'll go get it."

Julian had been our guest since his unexpected, island-style arrival in New York. So, as he went to his room, I wondered what, indeed, had he kept from that lurid expedition and brought with him into our home. My curiosity and dread were overwhelming. It rather chilled me to think that one of the objects from the Kahakuloa burial cave was, at this very moment, in our presence, in our apartment—separated, no doubt, a commodious distance of thousands of miles from Hawaii, but none-the-less harboring now an awesome ghostly property of some departed Hawaiian spirit.

Julian returned to the living room, and I quickly saw that it was a book. I breathed with a degree of relief.

"Here it is." He placed it in my hands. It was bound in calf-skin and appeared to be quite old. I could barely make out the gold imprint of its title, finally distinguishing the letters to read: *Paley's Philosophy*.

"This must be the book you didn't drop into the sea," I said, holding it off at a comfortable distance. "How do you suppose it got there?"

"Look inside," Julian answered abruptly.

Now what could I expect? Would the spirits of the war god Ku, or the more benign farmers' deity Lono, leap out from the covers? When

I opened the book, no such thing happened. Instead, I saw scrawled across the page preceding the frontispiece the name of my maternal great-great-grandfather.

"My god, this is impossible!"

"Not at all. I've speculated on this at some length. Your ancestor was one of the missionaries who took haole pala pala to the Sandwich Islands as a teacher. It so happened he had settled on the island of Maui. As you know . . ."

"But how do you suppose . . ."

"He must have been instructing one of the young chiefs of the family in philosophy, who happened to die while in possession of this book. Besides, his son, your great-grandfather, married into a chiefly family, didn't he? The young chief might have been a brother or an uncle of hers."

It was impossible not to feel dumbfounded. I turned another page of the old calf-bound book, and there it read: *The Principles of Moral and Political Philosophy,* by William Paley, D.D. A page or two before this, where the text began, and for many pages beyond that, copious notes had been scrawled in the margins, some in Hawaiian and some in English.

Julian had risen from the table to take another short flier around the living room. At one point he stopped short and exclaimed in a timorous voice, "On page ninety-one of the Paley you will find a reference made to caves."

I checked the page, found the reference, and proceeded to read it aloud: " . . . property in immovables continued . . . so long as a man's family continued in possession of a cave.'"

"You see, therefore," Julian said with tired triumph in his eyes, "I have brought the book to its natural heir. I am sorry about the other things, old man. Goodness knows where the trinkets and the tapa pieces are now."

Christmas Eve on Upper Fort Street

The misty rain, an *ua noe*, as the old Hawaiians called it, fell in diaphanous sheets between the three towering, sleek, impeccably designed buildings. It was late afternoon, nearing dusk really. In the light of this time of day and with this particular rain falling an aura, more curiously dreamlike than the everyday look of the handsome place, cast its magical spell over the high-rise surroundings of the Queen Emma Apartments on upper Fort Street in Honolulu. In the well appointed and sportily arranged apartment, stuffed to its bounds with every comfort, on the fourteenth floor of one of the three alii heaps of cement, hollow tile, and steel, I thought of many things:

Of sheafs of architectural drawings lying across sloped drawing boards, the work of draftsmen executing the brain child of a Nisei American architect of great talent; of conferences held in the temporary smoke-reeky sheds of construction firms, pondering costs of cement, structural steel, and hollow tile; of other rooms where other groups of men gathered in their hard-won decision-making roles; enclaves, meeting in joyless, immaculate, air-conditioned tombs discussing money—*big money:* the mortgage aspects of this modern miracle of three vast heaps rising above ground that had been only recently carpeted with growth and habitations having the quaint, artistic, tired look of a slum. These had grown as a layer over the posh kuleana of a handful of privileged island families after they had deserted the area. Then there was the image that came to mind of the hard-bitten, spiritually scarred bunch who sat around a political official's table discussing contracts, land values, and regulations of one sort or another; all this prettied up with semantic embellishments that might vaguely suggest a great society, a war on poverty, or an ephemeral pronunciamento called *progress*.

All this was happening in my thoughts in the fourteenth-floor apartment facing Vineyard and Nuuanu Streets where I was a guest for the evening, while the misty rain fell like the gauze fluttering across the proscenium arch of the Metropolitan Opera House in a version of Wagner's "Ring" staged in the 1940's.

The witchery of the mind's intentions can take it off in any direction at a time like this. In a second my thoughts were swept back thirty-five years in time. The svelte buildings fell to rubble, to nothing actually; the board meetings, architectural drawings, the meeting of the politicos, the noisy drone of cars moving along their six asphalt paths; even the rain evaporated, and for a moment it was Christmas Eve.

The smell of pak lan, ylang-ylang, and mei sui lan haunted all the air around Fort, Nuuanu, Vineyard, and School Streets. In huge wafts from surrounding gardens the heady, redolent assaults pushed their way across panax and hibiscus hedges and swept over verandahs, stole into livingrooms and down what seemed to a six-year-old the interminable lengths of a Victorian-styled bedroom hallway. In the moist cool air of December these fragrances were a sensate landmark of old Honolulu.

From the jungle surrounding the dark, silent domicile of Aunt Mary Foster, from the trees of pak lan that were giants in the Afong garden, and from the thicket of cherished, pampered horticultural darlings surrounding my grandfather's house, and from several other "yards" as they were called, the smells of night-blooming flowers spelled Christmas for me.

I waited with several of my boy cousins and our friends in the huge bedroom at the end of the hall which was called, when my father was a boy, *the dormitory*. It sat at the end of the long hall, the last in a row of seven bedrooms. Outside, the verandah reached its end at the north side of the house and engulfed like a giant lei three-fourths of the rest of the large, spreading island house.

"I'm goina get a pony," my cousin, Boy M., said with the jaunty air of an incipient gigolo. My secret was held close. This was not the time to spill it.

"I'm getting a set of golf clubs," said my cousin, Brooza, an oversized lad already well along toward an adulthood of obesity. "I'm goina play goff with my father," he added with an air of indolence and certainty peculiar to him alone of all my cousins.

Not yet, not yet. I won't tell them yet. The words spilled over and over in my brain like rushing waters pouring across a rocky riverbed.

We were awaiting the arrival of Santa Claus, impersonated that year by no less a person than the famed old town wit, Uncle Chester D., who was Japanese interpreter in the local courts by virtue of his having been born and raised in the ancient town of Kyoto.

Aunt E., Auntie A., and several other great aunts (there were scores of them filling the rooms of shadowy Victorian houses in those days) had planned a gala Christmas Eve party at the old Fort Street house. It was to be our last in the aging stronghold which had certainly reaped its harvests of revelry and grief since it had been built in 1881.

It turned out that they had planned for Uncle Chester to drive down the long lane leading in from Fort Street on a wagon packed with the expensive trinkets and playthings so adored by children at this time of year.

Heavily swathed in georgette, crepe-de-chine dresses, or assorted elaborately made holokus, my aunts and great-aunts and their accomplices in a high holiday mood of excitement made stately sorties throughout the house checking lighted candles. punchbowls, and recalcitrant over-exuberant children and servants.

Outside on the verandah at one point, I could hear Auntie Tweet-Tweet telling Great-aunt Battie, "What in heaven's name can be keeping Chestah!"

"Inu lii-lii, paha? He's stopped for a little drink, perhaps?"

"Kuli-kuli, Battie!" Auntie Tweet-Tweet scolded. "He promised not to take a single drink tonight until the last toy has been taken off that wagon."

And my Z—! I dared not think of it! It would, of course, be trotting like a young African prince alongside Boy's common little pony—both tied behind the wagon. It was the first knowledge I had that a wagon was to be used in this year's Christmas Eve celebration. This alone brought a thrill to a small boy's heart. The year before Santa had arrived in a lumbering, noisy, heavily decorated truck that had been borrowed for the evening from the local ice company.

Auntie Sha-Sha had promised faithfully before she left on her trip around the world after divorcing Uncle K. early that summer. She had promised! After doing so foolish a thing as asking a child what he would like her to send him from her global wanderings.

"I want a Zebra!" I had said with the authority and finality of a Greek statue when she asked what I wanted her to send me during her travels.

Floundering, I suppose, for a few moments after this avalanche had passed near her fluttering sense of credulity and having survived the holocaust, she said finally with her usual unshakable aplomb:

"Certainly! By all means! When I get to Africa, I'll try my best!"

What more did a small boy need than so positive a statement of assurance from an almighty adult? Gay laughter had floated like soft clouds passing over the ridgetops of Nuuanu through the rooms of the old Fort Street house where there had been a gathering of well-wishers and sympathetic relatives shortly before Aunt Sha-Sha began her journey.

"A Zebra!" someone had said, following the words with a burst of laughter. "You must be out of your mind, Sha-Sha!"

"I'll try to get it back to you by Christmas, darling," my aunt had said with a bravado that lifted the eyebrows collectively of an assemblage not given generally to this sort of thing.

I waited! How I waited! Each day, each week, each month accrued and massed up like grapenuts in a breakfast dish and stayed a hard, knotty cluster in my thoughts. A Zebra, no less! It would be the first one to be seen in Honolulu. Even at the Zoo there were no Zebra.

Where I would keep the proud, striped beast; how I would feed it was of small concern in my anticipations. After all, there was plenty of time to give thought to such ordinary, irksome necessities after the exotic creature arrived. The important thing was that Aunt Sha-Sha had promised to send me a Zebra, and being the kind of person she was—a gentle, thoughtful, child-loving but childless adult—I had every reason to believe she would follow through with her promise. Safely trusting of this gentle soul, I had waited, most of the time, in peace.

A pillow fight started by my cousin Timmy was stopped by Great-aunt Emily before it became a minor free-for-all.

"The very idea! A pillow fight at such a time as this! You ungrateful boys! I have half a mind to tell Santa Claus not to come!"

"Please! . . ." we wailed in an appealing chorus.

"All right, then! Not another sound from you! Understand?"

Heartily, submissively, gratefully we agreed, and then somewhat sheepishly we filed out of the dormitory and joined the other children scattered at various places throughout the vast old house.

The adults, some of them already well into their fourth or fifth okolehao old-fashioned (Hawaii's answer to Prohibition, superbly superior to bathtub gin), chattered their store of small talk. Children waited, painfully restive and unnaturally decorous now. White-suited houseboys prepared drinks and served them and quietly returned from these divertissements to the dining room where silver, crystal, and a conglomerate of Spode, Worcester and Royal Doulton were being neatly arranged around an enormous table. There was always a great feast, a "feed" as Aunt Emily called it, after the distribution of gifts to the children on Christmas Eve at the Fort Street house.

The high, ear-splitting scream of my cousin Eleanor announced the imminent arrival of the wagon. All the girl cousins joined in the squealing, and in a body swooped down the broad front steps which led up to the front doors—a noisy frothing mass of white dimity, voile, and madras, wide silk sashes of assorted colors splashing rude streaks through the cloud of white, like flashy mallards running riot through the ranks of a covey of Long Island ducklings.

Some impulse drove me indoors. I ran to the dining room and hid behind one of the commodes. Din-Din, the youngest of the houseboys, found me.

"Smalla you make all sam? Ellybody ou'sigh. You insigh. You go quick. Sanna Claus he come. Smalla you?"

He turned away in disgust to address Willie who carefully arranged the two salvers on a sideboard that would receive the plum puddings made faithfully from one of my great-grandmother's recipes.

"Dissy kit funny kine. Elly time him no all same nudda kit. Smalla him insigh—elly body elsie ou'sigh!"

Willie, an older man, had only smiled, and said nothing in answer to Din-Din's utterances of disgust.

I remained stubbornly fixed in my position behind the large piece of furniture indispensable to dining rooms of another era. This one had been made to order in Shanghai some decades before.

After what seemed hours, Aunt Emily began to search. "Where is—? Where is—?" Like a great roar at a football game, it seemed the house was filled with the sound of voices calling my name.

"Come and see what Santa Claus brought you! . . ."

The rooms of the house became filled again with squealing little girls clutching now great fish-eyed dolls and bits of tea sets and toy prams. Little boys raced through the rooms with baseball bats, new mitts smelling of freshly cured leather, and an assortment of footballs, volley balls, kiddie cars and wagons.

"Come and see what you got!" My cousin, Brooza, dragging behind him a superbly finished bag of golf clubs specially made for a boy, pulled me from my hiding place in the dining room. Protestingly I went to the verandah and found my way to the exuberant throng of adults, the men arrayed majestically in linen or pongee suits, and soft, billowing, multi-colored silks covering the frames of tall, heavy women.

"Here he is—here he is!" someone said.

"Where in hell's name have you been?" my father said with epic irritation. "Look at what Santa has brought you," he added in a tone registering gargantuan disgust that I could behave so ungratefully at a time like this.

Propped against the verandah balustrading was a huge teddy bear; and in his arms he clutched tightly a new football with my name printed across one side of it.

Uncle Chester D., partly freed from the ponderous swathings that had made him into Santa Claus, but still wearing the long white beard and looking now like a fantastic provincial imitation of Bacchus, drank lovingly from the fat glass that had been brought to him following the distribution of Christmas presents.

Down in the drive my cousin, Boy M., lovingly stroked the arching neck of a Welsh pony. I looked in vain, but there was no black and white striped beast the size of the pony tethered, as I had thought it would be, to the other side of the wagon.

"How about some sashimi," my hostess said. "You've been sitting here so quietly for so long."

How grateful I was to be brought back into present time at this moment. I could see now that the misty rain had passed on to lay its gentle moist kiss on the far off southern parts of Oahu. In the opposite direction I saw with relief the patriarchal, gaunt, and ageless form of Diamond Head, and gave my thoughts over to other matters, and let my taste buds be aroused by the anticipation of enjoying the inimitable flavor and texture of ahi sashimi.

Family Portraits

The old woman, stubbornly tenacious of life, lay dying in the big room upstairs. For a number of days her leave-taking of the world had filled the house with the futility of a dark and weighty shadow. From the miasma of her pain, her gradually ebbing consciousness, one statement recurred—the sound of it penetrating walls, escaping the closed doors, and coming through the monotony of groans with sharp distinction:

"Please, Laura, forgive me. Forgive me, Laura . . ."

Time and again the words had flowed out from the unconscious mouth, thin lips barely parted to give release to the tones of a once-splendid voice.

Until the last year or so Emily Christensen had lived her long life in a superb state of physical health. She was a big woman, as were all the Ayletts, with a commanding appearance and formidably structured will. She had practiced with deep conviction the philosophy of mind over matter; and for years she stood courageously against the assistance of professional medicine under any circumstance. It was her dedicated belief that sound thinking, regularity of habits, and prescribed eating would protect the body from the encroachment of disease, no matter how virulent it was. Emily Christensen had never consulted a doctor on her own behalf; and she had never been sick until this last year of her life, with the resultant collapse that had led to her being hospitalized.

So far as her aged sister, Rhoda Nahinu, was concerned, Emily was in the prime of her life at eighty-one when this thing happened. Rhoda had celebrated her ninety-second birthday a month or so before, and, though she had been blind for the past five years, she was still hale in spirit and mind. She looked upon Emily's collapse with the same indignant attitude that she would have given the fates should Emily have been sixty years younger. At eighty-one there was still some of the full ripeness of life to be tasted, so far as Rhoda Nahinu was concerned.

This sickness, which she would allow no one to properly define, had fallen quickly upon Emily Christensen, and, within a year after her second collapse, she was taken unconscious to the hospital.

"I want to go home instantly!" she had demanded after regaining consciousness enough to discover the pale green walls of her cubicle in the Maui General Hospital.

She had suffered a coronary attack. By all standards, considering her age and the rapid debilitation of her body in the past year or so, she should have remained in hospital for another month. But three days after her initial dramatic demand, which was followed by others, she was sent home to the large architecturally-nondescript house in Wailuku.

It was Rhoda Nahinu's house, but since Emily's establishment of residency (the move from Honolulu had not been enthusiastically welcomed by Rhoda) Emily had assumed mastership as easily as a seasoned pirate leader assumes the command of a vessel he has seized by conquest. "I have come to spend my last days with you, Sister Rhoda," Emily had said tersely and moved right in, fitting herself into the life of the old house—to embellish here, and distort there, the routines long established by Rhoda and her long-deceased husband, Isaiah Nahinu.

Lydia Smith, the patient all-abiding companion of Rhoda Nahinu, had written Charles Newton in Honolulu, twice, to come to Maui. In her first letter she had written that Aunt Emily had spoken of wanting to see her grandnephew, and would he please come. When they received his reply, full of excuses, saying that due to the push of business and the demands of his clients, he could not come right away, Aunt Emily, well fortified with the celebrated Aylett temper, had dictated the contents of a second letter in which she had simply commanded Charles Newton to make his appearance on Maui, or he could forget that she had ever promised to give him her father's private papers and the oil portraits of her grandparents, the High Chief and Chiefess Kekapuwai.

Charles had always wanted possession of his great-grandfather's papers, and above all the portraits of this pair of his noble Hawaiian ancestors, executed in the romantic style by a Frenchman who had passed through the islands as artist with a scientific expedition in 1841. After receiving his great-aunt's thundering ultimatum, which she had

had carefully dated November 1, 1959, he wrote speedily to say that he would go to Maui at the first moment he could leave his family and his office with impunity.

"Forgive me, Laura. Please, Laura, forgive me," Emily Christensen pleaded as Lydia Smith and Charles slipped from the hallway to the big sideboard in the dining room.

The plea held embarrassing connotations. It had kept Lydia Smith and the nurses dizzy with speculation. They had busied themselves for days, trying to ascertain a basis for so impassioned and lingering a cry of attrition.

"I suppose *you* know," Lydia Smith said with coy slyness as she offered Charles a drink. They were in the dining room at the sideboard where the liquor was kept.

"I'm afraid I was born some years after my grandmother's death. How could I know?" Charles answered tersely.

"But you have a way of knowing so much about the old folks and the old days. Aunt Rhoda always says you know more about the old days than she, and she actually lived them. Only the other day she reminded me that Kamehameha V was king when she was born!"

This rare acknowledgment of historic data was a departure on her part, so Charles ignored it. "I don't know anything about Aunt Emily's pitiful groans, but I can venture a guess," he said, and paused to note a childlike look of expectancy on Lydia's face. "She may have practiced adultery with my grandfather." He now wore the air of a judge, ruling in a divorce suit, and paused again to give Lydia a chance to absorb the impact of his statement. "She was often with him as his date at the Palace functions when he was on King Kalakaua's staff." Charles continued. "Something quite passionate may have occurred between them at that time. My grandmother, I've always been told, was too sickly to make public appearances with her husband." He paused. "Aunt Emily was a very beautiful woman, and I imagine quite sexy. From the things I've been told about my grandfather and his life at court, he must have been quite a hand with the ladies. The conditions were perfect for incubating adultery between Aunt Emily and my grandfather. I do know he lavished gifts on her."

"O dear, I hope Aunt Rhoda never hears about this!" Lydia sputtered unctiously.

"Don't worry, she probably knows a hell of a lot more than she lets out. Has *she* offered any explanation? Not on your life! These old ladies are very tight-lipped about some things." Charles stopped and softened his facial expression. "Remember, Lydia, that my statement is strictly a guess. You implied that I should know. Well, I've hazarded a guess. It may be the truth, or it may be entirely a falsehood."

Charles knew his words were tantamount to sacrilege in Lydia's mental housekeeping. He believed that, though she might, in the more recessed corners of her thinking, harbor views of disbelief in the sanctimonious facade behind which the old women barricaded themselves for the public eye, Lydia Smith would never dare under any circumstance disclose her doubts to anyone, let alone a member of the family.

Charles' abrupt and lusty speculation had frightened Lydia back into her customary pose of smiling and willing devotion to the ideals of the household. She had assumed a manner that implied she wouldn't ask again, ever—that old Aunt Emily could die with her mumbled secret for all she cared!

He excused himself after they had had two drinks and went to walk in the garden. He left the house by one of its back doors and took the walkway that led to the old chicken runs. The garden had been reduced in size, since he first came here as a child, to make way for the growth of the town. There was a municipal parking lot now where the cut flower and vegetable beds had once been, and a new flank of buildings, constructed upon the advice of Aunt Rhoda's attorney, rose from the southern borders of the lot's frontage.

He walked along the cracked sidewalk behind the guest house, now rented to a young haole couple who taught in the local schools, and met the sole remaining gardener, old Francisco of the blood-shot eyes. Charles was startled to notice how much Francisco had aged since he had last seen him two years ago. "Big yard for only one man to care for, Francisco."

"Me boy kokua som time—heem man now." Francisco was thinning out a plumeria tree, one of a long row planted many years ago along the walk to separate it from the kitchen garden.

"How is Banaay?"

"Heem okay. Work now por da gobernment."

Years ago Charles had climbed the many trees in the garden with the agile skinny Banaay in search of the ripest mangoes, avocado pears, and breadfruit.

"Where Banaay stay now?" Charles broke into pidgin.

"Heem stay down Ka'lui, by da place dey make plenny new house."

An image of the vast new subdivision under development in the Kahului section of the island flashed in Charles' thoughts. Kahului called up many memories. It was where the wharf sat, and where the inter-island ships had docked in the days of ocean travel between the various islands. He thought he might ask Lydia for the use of her car so he could go down and see what further changes had been effected upon the sleepy old face of Kahului. It was fast becoming the urban hub of Maui, robbing Wailuku of this preeminence which it had taken from Lahaina at the end of the last century.

His thoughts became increasingly jumbled. He tried to separate the past from the present, Maui from Oahu, and people like Francisco and Banaay and their posterity from himself, his children, his parents, and the old women inside the house. What had happened to Hawaii?

It was as though a great abstract explosion had occurred since World War II, scattering bits and chunks of the old life to the four winds, all of which had fallen back into place in a fantastically different complex of patterns.

The land boom! The building boom! A new crop of rich energetic people! A vast increase in doctors and lawyers, and, yes, architects. New public schools had popped up everywhere like mushrooms, some of them a credit to modern concepts of building, others puerile and ugly. He hoped the two complexes of school buildings he had been commissioned to plan on Oahu would always be considered good architecture.

New people had come to the islands from all directions. New industries had developed: garment manufacturing, tourism with its outcropping of tall hotels shadowing each other in Waikiki and occasionally surprising country beaches of the outer islands. A vast increase of military installations had taken place. Everyone's ears were bombarded by the roar of overhead flights of both civilian and military jets.

The blending of people of all races, the blending of their habits, beliefs, and genes had taken place with remarkable incidence in the islands of Hawaii. It was charged with a fast-moving cosmopolitan air, rid once and for all of its stultifying provincialism. One could live and breathe in the vastly less restricted atmosphere of the present day, freed of the terrible feeling he had suffered as a youth that one could never be released from the grasp of family and caste as it had been shaped by the forces that had organized the pattern of life in nineteenth-century Hawaii.

It was a beautiful land of beautiful people, strangers always observed, and, in general, Charles was inclined to agree. His aboriginal progenitors had harvested a rich and good way of life from these islands; and he knew that some of their legacy still lived on in the hearts of all islanders. Then a moment of doubt crept into the flow of thoughts: were he and his family, his aunts and his parents, and their circle of friends and relations really a part of new Hawaii? Or were they breathing anachronisms—figures in a tableau vivant, watching the scene from behind a thick plateglass window? They were, he knew, unwittingly caught in a labyrinthian design of history and tradition, caught in their role as a people by the tenacious pulls of pride, the fixed mortar of prejudice and habit.

He walked aimlessly, turning over in his mind these thoughts, and came into a section of the garden he had always loved. For a moment he imagined he heard the groaning lament of Aunt Emily's agonies. He looked up to find that he was below her bedroom. She had chosen that room as her own when she had come "to stay," because it looked down on the lavish tangle of vegetation that grew in the shadowed recesses of the garden, and because, as she had said contentedly, it was the largest room on the second floor of the old house, having been Uncle Isaiah's bedroom until he died.

From the entire crop—a large one—of grandnephews and grandnieces, it had been Charles' lot to spend more time than any of his cousins, with this peculiar and fascinating woman, their Great-aunt Emily. Members of the family in Honolulu had thought it would be a good idea if he went up for a few days—a kind of emissary of goodwill and devotion on behalf of themselves. Their premise was that Aunt Emily craved a little attention. Aunt Rhoda had established for them the precedent that Aunt Emily was also imperishable. It was impossible to accept the idea that she might be dying. In their habitual way of thinking, the old house and the old women stood for eternity. So now at Aunt Rhoda's command, Charles had come to Maui to join the lonely "death watch," as Great-aunt Emily, flattened now onto her big four-poster bed betrayed her agonies. Of all her worldly possessions, he wanted nothing more from his great-aunt than the papers and the paintings she had always promised to give him "in time."

It was no easy matter for him to leave his wife and three children and his architectural commissions behind in Honolulu to come join this macabre scene on Maui. He was devoted to his family and to the aesthetic and functional pulls of his profession. They were comfortably removed from the life of his great-aunts and the old house in Wailuku, and were a solid barricade against some of the memories that flushed up in his mind on occasion which harked back to the days he had spent with the old women as a child and youth.

For years he had stayed away from the old place (as much as decency allowed) paying only short official visits to his great-aunts whenever business or a holiday respite took him to the island of Maui.

His memories were too filled with confused images and a persisting rancor, so far as the old house was concerned, to make going there now, under any circumstance, just another of those unpleasant little duties which his tradition-ruled mind drove him to fulfill. It was really the old women who engendered his hostile recollections; yet the house itself, its gray-shingled exterior, its ridiculous second-story balcony running halfway across the front that faced Main Street, its oppressive furnishings and appointments, stubbornly remained in his thoughts as the chief symbol of the torments of his first visits to the island of Maui.

Every summer when Charles was young Aunt Emily had gone to spend two months with her sister, and Charles, as the favorite grandnephew, a captive in the surrealist web of Aunt Emily's affection, went along too. It had been her contention that Charles could gain a flavor of life not available to him in the simpler, more crowded surroundings of his parents' home. She had looked upon the life of Jack Newton and his family with regal and autocratic disapproval.

To begin with, Jack and Mary Newton had too many children. Endowing the world with seven squalling and eternally hungry siblings, in this day and age, was an insult to common decency. It was true *her* parents had produced a family of eight, but they lived in an age that welcomed the prospect of large families.

She had had no children, and neither had her sister Rhoda. Her sister Anne had had five (bad enough); and Laura, three. The twins, Hattie and Victoria, had each had only one child. There was no need for Emily Christensen to give the enormous families her brothers, Charles and Francis, had produced the least consideration, for they married "beneath" them, and as such were outside the pale of Emily's concern. She had simply struck them from her mind as a source of either pleasure or disdain.

But in the case of Jack and Mary Newton, it was pure indecency for them to have brought so many children into the world at a time when everyone else, except poor working-class people of course, had small families. Mary, after all, was a Hubbard from the well-known family of that name on Maui. She had inherited property and shared the income of a large trust left by her haole grandfather, old Bently Hubbard, who had been an original partner in the Maui Sugar Plantation Company, Limited. Mary should have had more sense. Emily's brothers' wives, being simple Hawaiian women of the people, what could you expect of them but to produce scores of children like wanton sows! "Only people of this sort, and the Japs and Chinks, have large families now-a-days," Aunt Emily was fond of saying. "They simply don't know any better. But Mary Hubbard Newton, of all people, to perform like a common brood mare!"

In spite of her frequently expressed hatred for the Hubbards, she respected them for their money and "good blood." Often she had drummed into young Charles that his parents' fall from the aristocratic pinnacle of rich landowning Hawaiians was due to their having so many children. And above all, it was certainly the reason they were so poor. By taking the child on these annual jaunts to Maui, she had felt a heroic sense of rescuing Charles from the encroaching proletarian vortex into which her nephew, Jack Newton, was allowing his family to be pulled.

For all his misgivings, Charles had sometimes invited remembrances of the old house and its accoutrements, and the peculiar way of life and thinking of the people who had lived in it. Ignorance and refinement, kindness and cruelty, generosity and frugality: all existed side by side in the old house. Over all there hung a threatening moral sense that was steeped in the Victorian ideal, but which was somehow uniquely imbued with the overtones and shadings wrought upon it by the local ethos.

Aunt Emily could swear to her heart's content in this house, or be a great lady; Aunt Rhoda could vacillate in her speech from the local patois called pidgin to the use of the excellent English spoken with a British accent in the manner of their father, the late Judge Aylett of Maui. They could hate certain people with the force of a thunderstorm, and yet be cloyingly sweet if the same people happened to pay a visit with baskets of flowers, or fruit, or fresh country eggs and butter brought down from the cool upland slopes of Haleakala. It was as though their child-like glee contained some magical property that would dissolve the hostility they may have expressed only moments before. They hated people with a tireless irrational passion, especially Hawaiians of the working class, and Orientals.

The house had survived what Charles Newton thought to be an era of the grossest provincialism Hawaii had known: the fifty-year interval following the overthrow of the Monarchy to the time of World War II. For this, he was proud of it. But it did not excuse it, in his mind, for being an absolute travesty of good sense, architecturally speaking, like some of the giddy concoctions of the famed Rhode Island summer resort. Aunt Emily had been responsible for the final touch of irrationality, after she came "to stay," by having the gray-shingled exterior of the mansion painted a blinding white. At least to Charles Newton, this was an expression of madness since the hot dry climate made Wailuku a dusty town, and since white tended to further dramatize the house as a swollen misshapen architectural mass.

In spite of its stubborn survival into the age of rockets, cold wars, and Metrecal, which gave it the proud irrefutable authenticity and strength of a historic document, it was still a house of closed doors and furtive whisperings, a house where the harshest words of criticism—a kind of pathological and systematized practice of character assassination—had occurred over the years like a ritual. It had stood in the center of the little town for over seventy years, a powerful bastion of the holier-than-thou legend, and now a dark and harsh reminder of an age that was passing rapidly from the Hawaiian scene.

Charles had passed Aunt Rhoda's glass-covered greenhouse, her "fernery"—now somewhat dilapidated—and settled into the cool shade of a large sterculia tree. In the corner of the squarish area, in loosely defined planting beds, he saw again the lovely tangle of anthurium, dieffenbachia, and other aroidaeaceous plants growing under three Samoan coconut palms and a small forest of tree fern. It comforted him that this section of the garden had never lost its character; he imagined it might have remained essentially the same as it had been in Uncle Isaiah's time—a nineteenth century Hawaiian-style garden into which plants of elegantly shaped leaves with strange coloration and texture, or plants that produced dramatic unseemly blooms had been placed with a pleasant, almost ridiculous simplicity. It was in such contrast to the rooms of the big house, crowded as they were with dark and dust-covered furnishings.

What would Uncle Isaiah have thought of the new Hawaii? For that matter, what would the High Chief Kekapuwai have thought of the new Hawaii? Charles smiled to himself. They would have loved it—the roar and bustle of change, the chains of provincialism shattered, and people at last seeing themselves in some relation to the rest of the world.

The picture of Aunt Emily flattened onto her big four-poster bed, unconscious of her suffering and mumbling her futile and comfortless plea for forgiveness, broke rudely into his thoughts.

When he had come to Maui the day before, it had been too late to talk with Aunt Emily; she had fallen into what proved to be her final period of unconsciousness. Just before this happened she had sternly given orders to her nurse that her nephew Charles was to have the two paintings and the cardboard box which she had packed and secured neatly with the assistance of her maid, Mary Souza, immediately after she had been returned from the hospital.

Aunt Emily had always postponed these gifts to Charles, saying vituperously at one time past: "You can have my photographs and my father's papers some day. You can also have those oil portraits. Not now! Some day! I hate them! I've always hated them! He was no good! The High Chief Kekapuwai was *no good!* He drank too much! His wife—she was your great-great-grandmother—she was an old boozer, too! They always drank brandy! Squandered a fortune on brandy. My mother was brought up by the missionaries. They took her away from her parents before *she* was ruined."

Charles had wondered at the time why Aunt Emily had bothered to reveal all this to his wife Helen, for this cantankerous speech had been delivered in a moment of great excitement during one of her visits to Honolulu. And it was the occasion of her first meeting with Helen. "An odd stiff creature," she had whispered to Charles, "but solid!" Being haole, and coming from New England, greatly enhanced Helen's place as a human being in Aunt Emily's estimation.

One of the paradoxes in his great-aunt's life was that she both enjoyed and hated being part-Hawaiian. She had kept these large oil portraits of the High Chief Kekapuwai and his wife for years in the carriage house of her home on Lunalilo Street in Honolulu. Kept them out of sight, was Charles' contention. He knew also, from the family talk, that Uncle Isaiah and Aunt Rhoda had wanted those paintings for years. Uncle Isaiah particularly, for he wanted them to hang with portraits of his noble ancestors on the walls of his big house in Wailuku. Aunt Emily would never give them up. She had got possession of the paintings after her mother's death and had shipped them to Honolulu. They had been uncrated and left to sit in the hayloft of her old carriage house, ignominious, and out of sight. Whenever anyone would ask her about the paintings she grew florid with anger. "Those paintings are no concern to anyone but myself," she would say later to herself, or to her cook or houseboy. "Nobody's concern but mine!"

Charles walked out of the luxuriously-planted section of the garden and went to explore the strip that ran parallel to High Street. It was many years since any of his time spent with the old ladies had permitted him a period of exploration or time for reflection, especially in the garden.

The great mango trees, three of them, were still there. He remembered those early summer mornings, long ago, when he had been made to come out and pick up fruit and leaves that had fallen during the night. How helpless he had been then against the roaring implacable stream of orders that had been issued by his childless aunts!

He noticed that the beds of palapalai fern that were planted against the foundations of the house still grew profusely under the shade of the mango trees. It was a graceful plant, palapalai—something in its look pulled one back to neolithic times. Aunt Rhoda had brought the original root clusters down from the kukui tree forests in Iao Valley when the house was first built and here they had grown and multiplied during all these years.

There were elements about the old place that were filled with charm and grace. It was indeed a repository of Hawaiian history, and had become over the years a landmark. But why had the old women seemed always to be so cruel, so unyielding in their bitterness that it poisoned the whole life of the place? He returned to the Hawaiian garden and sat on the granite bench which rested against a stone wall. He gave his thoughts once again to Aunt Emily.

He had become increasingly aware of her feelings of inferiority. With no attempt at subtlety or caution she had sometimes revealed that she must have suffered a life-time of displeasure over her miscegenated origins. "Father was English, a fine Englishman. His table was elegant and refined. If you wanted to eat Hawaiian-style in his house, you ate on the mats out on the lanai with our wards and the servants. We had plenty of them. Father was a judge. He brought home dozens of the wards of the court and protected them under his own roof—as if he didn't have children enough of his own to feed and clothe. There were eight of *us*," she had said to Helen.

At other times she had extolled the virtues of cousins, nieces or nephews who had married "white," always careful now to disguise the pushing, gnawing thing that seemed to have been aching within her by not making her approval too pointedly. She scarcely spoke of her mother—Great-grandmother, Kilikina Aylett was a dim nonentity in Aunt Emily's conversations. It was enough to say that she was sweet and gentle and patient, "as all mothers should be." He remembered conversations with Aunt Emily on the lanai which swept across the entire front of her charming old house on Lunalilo Street in Honolulu. He had probed her on many occasions for information concerning her parents and her early years. Sometimes she would talk a great deal; at other times she would be rude and sullen.

Painfully he remembered now the charming house with its bungalow latticings and squarish form, which had been torn down when the trust company in charge of Aunt Emily's affairs had suggested she build cottages on the huge lot to increase her income. Six little dumpy oblong dwellings, stained a dark brown and trimmed with white, and a seventh, a larger one facing Lunalilo which she occupied, had sprung up like weeds in place of the large white bungalow and the great sweep of green lawn that had extended from its entrance to the street. Charles could still reassemble this picture of the white bungalow in his mind's eye to perfection.

The surfaces of its exterior walls and the verandah floors were subjected annually to new coats of paint. Furnishings were sparse but tasteful, preciously arranged on hardwood floors that glistened with a high and scrupulously-applied polish. Her cook and the number-two boy went about their duties in glossy white uniforms. Her cats, who bore elf-like names such as Tinker Bell and Peter Pan, were great, white, carefully brushed Persians. She had allowed only the most delicate-looking of maiden hair fern and such orchids as phalaenopsis with their decidedly chaste appearance to be hung in the conservatory.

Charles had always been struck with the incongruence between Aunt Emily's behavior and thought, and the character of her house— the one a mastodon of harsh words, the other as precious as a miniature poodle. There was a rumour in the family that her late husband, who had been some twenty years her senior, had purposefully kept to sea after retirement might have been inviting, in order to escape the studied effeminacy of his wife's house.

And though she had been affected emotionally by the use of Hawaiian food in her father and mother's household, how she loved to eat the native foods. This love increased rather than diminished as she grew older and older. Even in the pristine elegance of her house in Honolulu, she had occasionally indulged herself in an orgy of Hawaiian foods in the old-fashioned manner that employed the fingers as eating utensils. Several types of raw fish fixed with seaweed, raw squid, lomi salmon, kalua pig—even akinaau, a flushed raw-beef liver delicacy prepared with a rich kukui nut paste and hot peppers, would be laid out on her table. She would devour poi with great lunging movements of her head and mouth, lustily dipping two fingers into the pinkish-gray ooze with each added bite of flesh or seaweed. This indulgence she practiced in solitude or in the company of one or two of her devoted cronies, as genteel in their demeanor as Aunt Emily was not, but given to the same secret lust for an occasional feast of Hawaiian delicacies which they held as a sure mark of the tainted barbarism of their ancestry, best kept to themselves as a bad habit— like smoking opium.

While studying the graceful arching chartreuse fronds of a tree fern, the paintings emerged again from some corner of his thoughts. The French painter, who might have been one of the pupils of the great Jacques Louis David, Charles felt, had used mountains and tree ferns in the background of the portraits. It seemed to him, that in his first impression of the paintings, the backgrounds had captured his spirit, lifted him up above and beyond the present, and carried him to the distant times of drumbeats and the hula alaapapa. The portrayal of island mountains, the romantic delicate treatment of the native fern, a cibotium, had stayed fixed in his memory. Where were the paintings now? He had neglected to ask since his arrival. It had just slipped his mind.

The late afternoon sunlight penetrated the branches of a nearby breadfruit tree and those of the sterculia, and scattered streaks of light over the garden. He was, for a moment, caught in the spell of his memory of the paintings and the sleepy, sensuous mood of the garden. Again he experienced waves of recollection, and he gave his thoughts to Aunt Rhoda.

She was different, or at least she seemed to be. She had married a Hawaiian, a stately giant, as given to the wearing of fashionable clothes as he was to oratory. If she had misgivings over her "Hawaiian side" she never voiced them. One had the feeling that her life with Isaiah had been full of happiness and reward; that he had loved her passionately, and gave indications of this in many ways. Aunt Rhoda had always told how, whenever Uncle Isaiah returned from the legislative session in Honolulu where he served as a member of the House of Nobles in the time of King Kalakaua, he brought her presents: a Chinese vase, a handsome new chair, a gilded mirror, many bottles of scented water, and bolts and bolts of expensive cloth that came to the islands from Europe and China. One time, he brought her a frisky pacer, a bay stallion, which he named "Rosebud" because, as Jack Newton had told his son Charles, the small cerise buds of a native rose plaited into the fronds of palapalai fern was Aunt Rhoda's favorite lei. If Uncle Isaiah wished to get drunk and to roister with lusty companions, he would go to the beach cottage, called "The Fishery"—out of deference, he would say, to Aunt Rhoda, who despised drunken revelry. Rhoda was the only one of the beautiful daughters of the old judge and his Hawaiian wife who had chosen a pure Hawaiian mate.

"Isaiah was vile-tongued," Aunt Emily would love to say when she felt like taunting her elder sister. "A good man, but given to foul language and a bad temper. Why, you were 'barked at,' Sister Rhoda, enough to last a woman two lifetimes." To this Aunt Rhoda would answer a low pitched, tolerant, "Oi'a no hoi," which said, if given the proper inflection, that whatever Aunt Emily had wished to accomplish in making these judgments of Isaiah's character, she could plumb go to hell so far as Rhoda Nahinu was concerned. This was ample proof to Charles that his Aunt Rhoda was as fixed in her belief in her husband's goodness as monumental Diamond Head is fixed to the southern end of Waikiki.

Charles believed that Aunt Emily could not seriously discredit her brother-in-law, for he was an excellent man—an old-world Hawaiian aristocrat, who, by some exertion of will and intelligence, had died a man of considerable property. Charles was acquainted enough with his great-aunt to know that she never totally disparaged persons of property.

The portrait of Isaiah Nahinu, which since his death had hung over the great safe that had been inserted into the wall of his office-library, bespoke a man who might well thunder and punish the dark air of his house with "foul language," but never in the sense that Aunt Emily wished to imply. In saying such a thing about Isaiah Nahinu, Charles had thought Aunt Emily was projecting into the image of the deceased man her own propensity to use "foul language." He suspected that she may also have been ignorant of the intrinsic differences in expressions that are profane, on the one hand, and obscene, on the other. It was his feeling that some of Aunt Emily's verbal explosions were simply obscene, while Uncle Isaiah's may have been less colorfully profane.

Charles had always regretted, with a deep sense of having been denied something of great importance in his formation an adult human, that Uncle Isaiah had died of a stroke years before it was possible for Charles to have known him. He had had to make the acquaintance of this man, who looked out from his portrait with the commanding appearance of a lusty savant, from biographical tidbits tossed out carelessly in the conversations of his great-aunts, and upon occasion, by his father, who had been a young crony of Uncle Isaiah's in the last days of his life.

It was time to go in—to leave the one remaining corner of the Nahinu house and garden that was in all respects attractive and, yes, even comforting. He would ask Lydia Smith about the paintings. It was time he saw them, and made arrangements for getting them to Honolulu. He could leave tomorrow. There was no sense in staying any longer.

When Charles had gone out into the garden, Lydia Smith waited until Aunt Rhoda took her afternoon nap, before she made a telephone call:

"Is this Honey's Restaurant? Is Mr. Smith there?" She cupped her right hand over the receiver and waited. Impatience made her twitch. Her face took on a pinkish flushed look that gave her brown skin a pleasant roseate cast. This was the second call she was making to her cousin, Aylett Smith.

"Hello, Cousin Aylett," she said anxiously. "Lydia here, eh? I must tell you that Charley Newton's here. He came late yesterday. He's come for the paintings."

She was silent for a moment, her impatience growing. "He's come for the paintings," she repeated. "Aunt Emily gave them to him, you know. But Aunt Rhoda says he has no right to them. They belonged to her mother."

Resolutely Lydia assured her cousin Aylett Smith, who was one of Francis Aylett's illegitimate children, that the paintings were his as soon as he brought the money to her. She could manage Aunt Rhoda. She had insisted that if he paid five hundred apiece for the pictures, he was getting a bargain. And, of course, it was necessary for him to keep the whole transaction under cover, and to keep the paintings out of sight until Aunt Rhoda died—which would not be too long from now, considering how very old she was.

Aylett Smith owned the highly profitable restaurant and bar down in Kahului, which he had playfully named Honey's in honor of his wife. He was Lydia's first cousin in a legal sense, their fathers being brothers, but everyone on the island, of the old set, knew that Aylett was one of Francis Aylett's "catch colts," and that he was born a couple of years before Esther Maialoha had married Keoki Smith.

Lydia had called him the first time and played upon her cousin's pride in being, in truth, an Aylett by offering him the paintings; and since he used the same bookkeeper who handled Aunt Rhoda's accounts (an intimate friend of Lydia's) she knew the kind of profits Aylett Smith made from the operations of his bar. He was about the only one around in the family now who could afford to pay a decent price for the large historic paintings.

In closing her telephone conversation, Lydia whispered to her cousin that the paintings were now safely out of the house and in the old garage far to the rear of the guest cottage and the big house. He could come around later in the evening—around eleven perhaps—and bring one thousand dollars. "In cash, if you please," she insisted. "No reflections on your banking habits, Aylett dear, but we must be careful and manage to keep all this a secret." He had agreed, but insisted on a statement of receipt. "Just anything, so long as it describes the pictures, and indicates they are paid for with solid cash."

Lydia had calculated her answer to Charles Newton should he ask about the paintings. She had carefully maneuvered Aunt Rhoda toward a point of view that held, in effect, that Charles had no right to take the paintings away. They were, in a sense, as much Aunt Rhoda's property as they were Aunt Emily's. She had merely had custody of the paintings for all these years; she had no business, no moral right, to give them to Charles, now that she faced the end of life.

"But when Sister Emily recovers," Aunt Rhoda had said the night before as Lydia prepared her bed, "she will want to know if Charles has the pictures. It will cause an argument."

"The doctor has said for three days now, that she is very close..." Lydia said.

"My poor sister," Aunt Rhoda had said in a piteous quavering voice.

Served her right, to be dying in this way, Lydia had thought vindictively. She had been a bully, a contentious and mean bully, all her life. Lydia had waited hopefully for at least fifteen years for the day Emily Christensen departed permanently from Aunt Rhoda's house.

It was after this conversation with Aunt Rhoda that Lydia had conceived the plan of offering the historic paintings to Aylett Smith. She knew how desperately he reached out for his identity as an Aylett. It was a fixation with him. He was proud and vulgar. He would do anything to embellish his life with the trappings of identity and position. With the cunning of a long-abiding and faithful retainer—full of wisdom that grew from years of silence and submission—Lydia Smith knew that Aylett Smith would leap at the chance of possessing the portraits of the alii couple. She knew that he would quickly appraise the prestige value they could have, hanging on the walls of his shapeless, but large, new house, high above the town in the Waikapu hills. What a slap in the face to Charles Newton and the whole pompous clan of Ayletts, Newtons, Hubbards, Pittmans, and Hulls; every last one of them clutching their ancestry and money, like greedy monkeys hoarding the peanuts someone had thrown into their cage.

Satisfied that the arrangement she had just made with her cousin was secure, Lydia poked her head into Aunt Rhoda's room and saw that the aged woman was still safely asleep. She couldn't possibly have heard the telephone conversation. Lydia's body experienced a curious feeling of excitement. Her arms and fingers tingled, her legs felt light and springy.

At this moment of her triumph, Lydia was too preoccupied to hear the soft scuffle of Mary Souza's go-aheads just outside the library door. Lydia was ignorant of Mary's having stood quietly outside the screen door leading from the hall into the library, hearing every word that she had spoken.

Charles entered the house at the front door, and found Mary Souza rushing upstairs with a tray.

"Do you know where Miss Smith is, Mary?"

Middle-age and the heavy duties implied in giving service to so spirited a woman as Aunt Emily had not depreciated Mary's appearance to any pronounced degree, Charles noted.

"I doh know wheah she stay. I nevah see um dis aftah-noon," Mary said quickly. She had not decided yet, where or how she should tell Charles about the telephone conversation she had overheard.

"How's Aunt Emily?"

"She okay. Da doctah been come dis aftah-noon for geev um som madcin. She steel talkin to hersalf." Mary rested the tray on the bannister and registered impatience with a loud sigh.

"I'll be up to look in on her soon. After I see Miss Smith."

Mary scooted up the remaining stairs before Charles could find a reason to detain her again. He went into the first of the double parlors and saw that it was empty. His eyes scanned the room and beyond to the second parlor where the old square piano sat, and then, beyond, to the dining room which made up the third great room occupying this side of the house. The library and Uncle Isaiah's study, which he had used also as his office, a large bathroom, and a servant retreat made up the other half of the first floor of the house.

Had laughter and kindness crept from this house only after Uncle Isaiah's death? It was so lifeless, like a great abandoned stage set, Charles imagined, as he let his eyes wander over the contents of the large, high-ceilinged rooms.

Here still hung the ridiculous pictures: lithographs of scenes from Greek and Roman mythology, flower paintings, and here and there an enlarged photograph of an island scene. A naked slave girl with long tresses, her private parts hidden by an enormous water jug, looked down from her place on the wall with pleading hopeful eyes; marble busts and bronze figurines, sad imitations of Verrochio and Cellini, sat on pedestals or small tables. The stuffed fox terrier "Jerry"—he had been Uncle Isaiah's favorite pet—sat gloating in his place under the square piano. A pair of love birds were arranged on a small branch under a glass bell, a large sulphur-crested parrot sat on his pedestal near a bouquet of ceramic flowers atop the old piano. These were watched over from above by an owl, a pueo or native owl, who had been fashioned to assume the appearance of being hungry and in flight by a clever taxidermist of another age. With wide-eyed and fierce determination, the owl looked down on the preserved remains of the avian flock below him. He was held in his position three or so feet above the piano by long wires that were suspended from the ceiling.

Charles could not quite reconcile the image of Uncle Isaiah in acceptable relationship to these rooms. The shuttered decorum, the sentimentality, the gross and offensive lack of aesthetic sensibilities, the dustiness, were difficult to relate to the brilliant and life-loving Isaiah Nahinu. Charles' Aunt Emily Kennedy, sister of Jack Newton, always vowed that Uncle Isaiah had required the service of crystal finger bowls after each meal of the day. Was it possible that this flamboyant congregation of household possessions had been brought together and placed by Uncle Isaiah, that in his life as master of the house the rooms could have held a welcoming air of expansiveness, generosity, and imagination; that now, unmoved, unfreshened, embalmed in lint and neglect by unwilling housekeepers—the bright warmth and vitality of the host removed for all time—the rooms had wrapped themselves into this disconsolate and miserable imitation of what Uncle Isaiah had lived with?

Had Aunt Emily's nihilism provided the final touches in making the house a crypt of sullen memories? But even before she had come "to stay," the house had assumed some of its present-day character for architecturally it had always been ugly, and its furnishings downstairs had always seemed funny.

The bedrooms upstairs were different, each with its four-poster bed or beds spread over with elaborately designed kapas, simple dressers, night stands, a rocker or two, and lauhala mats spread across the floors. They were uncluttered, miraculously so, considering the dark amorphous incrustation of the rooms below.

He heard the sound of steps on the verandah, and then soon after saw Lydia scurrying down the hallway carrying a small parcel toward the kitchen. He rose quickly and called out after her: "May I see you for a moment, Lydia?"

So the moment had come, Lydia thought. He wants to see his precious paintings. "I've got to get Aunty up and help her dress," she called back. "I'll see you later."

Her words hung on the dark walls, giving an even more distasteful look to the thickly varnished surfaces. He left the parlor and went upstairs to his room. He had been given the front south bedroom, the one he had occupied as a child when he had paid his first visits to Maui.

The bay window looked down into the space of garden that separated the house from Main Street. Charles looked below onto the great clumps of bird-of-paradise, an impressive mass of gray-green leaves accented sporadically by the erect spikes of flower stems, atop of which sat the stiff bird-like cluster of orange and blue streaked blossoms shooting out like a gentle flame from the torpedo-shaped bracts in which the petals were held secure. Aunt Rhoda had had the sole bird-of-paradise on Maui for many years. In the beginning, she had had a cage of heavy wire, complete with a small locked gate, built over the precious clump. It was a spectacle for the townspeople to come and see when the first flowers appeared. "My goodness," Aunt Rhoda had sighed every time she told the story, "everyone wanted a flower or a keiki, or both."

On either side of the front entrance, two Chinese magnolias stood like exotic sentinels, filling the long still nights with heavy fragrance when their blooms appeared. A huge arbor framed the front gate between the two magnolia trees, a rather ugly wooden support for a luxuriant tangle of stephanotis. In bloom, the vines held the townspeople in awe. The masses of waxy, off-white flowers covered the entire frame and spotted the nearest branches of magnolia with fragrant palest ivory clusters.

A thicket of ixora, producing perfumed white blossoms, grew against the bay window of the front parlor, and across the walk an enormous aglaia, the mei sui lan of China, screened the entire area of the verandah from view of the street. The fragrance of its tiny round yellow flowers, held together in neat bunches, infused a paradisiacal aura to the warm nights during the blooming period.

What in the hell was on Lydia's mind? Her sharp terse reply of a moment ago came back to him. To avoid irritation, Charles again gave his consideration to the scene below:

Main Street. It was actually called Main Street. How out of place this seemed in Hawaii. And yet, was this not a composite of streets, buildings, people, caught in an offshoot-phenomena of civilization called the small town just as Lewis had described it in his famous novel? It was essentially the same kind of place. Different people, with a different cultural background and climate—that was all.

He felt drowsy and decided to nap. How dull it all seemed, and how futile! Sleep would be a blessing. When he woke up he'd get the paintings and the box of papers and leave immediately. He would go to a hotel—the one on the beach down at Kahului. It was too much to expect of himself to spend another night here. Yet he knew he could not; he knew it would hurt Aunt Rhoda if he did this. But why the hell should he care about this. Hadn't he suffered enough of the tyranny these old women had dished out relentlessly to their younger relatives during those endless summer days he had spent here as a youth?

Aunt Emily's groans sounded again throughout the house. She had stubbornly emerged from the merciful sleep induced by a large dose of morphine. Lydia had told Charles the night before that Aunt Emily was being given regular dosages of the pain-killing drug.

After removing his shoes and his outer clothing, Charles put on his dressing gown. He pulled back the elaborate Hawaiian quilt, a kapa covered with the design of the Hawaiian flag, and stretched out across the width of the massive four-poster koa bed.

Why these terrible groans? Why should the old woman suffer so and keep uttering her humiliating, agonized, guilt-steeped plea? Hadn't she suffered enough? Hadn't they all suffered enough? Loss of fortune, dope addiction, alcoholism, psychotic breakdowns, and a terrible sense of bewilderment had plagued the family for years. Some of it, if told, would puzzle the imagination of an Edgar Allen Poe.

This room for instance. This very room. The first time he had ever come to Maui, they had come by way of Lahaina. It was very late when they arrived after driving the twenty-five miles to Wailuku from the far western tip of Maui Island where Lahaina lay. A mere child of seven, he had been put alone into this enormous bedroom.

"How silly for you to be afraid, Charles," Aunt Emily had cajoled. "Aunt Rhoda has put you in the very room that our old Queen occupied when she came to Maui. She slept in this very bed."

And this was enough to thoroughly secure the encroachment of child fears. Queens were sacred creatures, austere and indomitable. In the large photograph signed by the Queen, which hung in his parents' bedroom at home, she was swathed in great billows of dark cloth, and she looked out from the image of herself with a sad and disapproving expression. Dead queens and the beds they slept in were enough to curdle the blood and the spirit he had inherited from indigenous ancestors, who had been artists in formulating the veiled and shadowy figments of superstition. As he let himself be carried into the labyrinths of the past, he heard a light knock at the door. He sat up.

"Come in," he said, thinking it was Lydia.

Instead, the round sturdy form of Mary Souza appeared in the doorway. "I no can talk long time. Bime bye she come." She furtively scanned the hallway and stairs. "Da pitchas no stay. Lydia take um away. Hanty Ameely, she say um for you! Dose pitchas for you!"

"What are you trying to tell me, Mary?"

"Dat son-um-a-beetch Lee-dia like sell um."

"You mean Lydia Smith wants to sell the paintings?" He paused and wrapped his dressing gown around himself more securely. "She can't do that. Those paintings belong to me. Where are they—do you know?"

"She teenk I doan know. I know. Mary not one god-dam fool. She put um insigh da garadge an wrap um up wit ole blankeet. Tonight da dirdy bugga Smitty come gat um. He's going buy da pitchas foah five hundred dollahs one!"

"Does Aunt Rhoda know this?"

"She doan know notting."

"Thank you, Mary, thanks a lot for telling me."

He showered quickly after Mary left, put on a light-weight shirt, and hurried downstairs. Aunt Rhoda had been awakened and put into one of the silk holokus she always wore in the evening, and sat at her perch near the front parlor bay window, looking for all the world like an ancient shrivelled bird of prey.

"Who is it?" she asked in a plaintive voice.

He went and kissed her cheek. It was cool and freshly scented with toilet water.

"It's you, Charlie," she said with her habitual chuckle.

"Yes. Did you rest well?"

"O, yes, well enough. Not much else for a blind old lady to do." In her blindness, Aunt Rhoda seemed even more like a large and patient bird.

"Has Lydia come down? I want to ask her about the paintings."

Aunt Rhoda moved almost imperceptibly in her chair. "Lee-dia," she said, giving the name a more Hawaiian pronunciation, "is having her bath. She'll be down soon."

Charles scanned again the big room. His curiosity seemed never to be satisfied by any scrutiny he had given this section of the house—as though some hidden assault upon his aesthetic sense made him want to excuse his memory from ever performing the duty of cementing knowledge of the rooms' furnishings into a clear and sustaining recollection. The figure of Isaiah Nahinu rose up: the voice, the great height, the handsome face, the debonair manner, his thirty suits and twenty-five pairs of shoes, crystal fingerbowls at every meal, his reputation as a host. The figment did not logically assume a place within the rooms as they were now.

Aunt Rhoda cleared her throat and made a strange sound, the product of age and anxiety. Charles listened.

"I feel sorry that you are taking those pictures of my grandparents." She waited and cleared her throat again, turning her sightless gaze from one side of the room to the other, forcing herself through her sightlessness to ascertain the exact position Charles occupied in the room. "Isaiah and I always wanted those paintings. Isaiah was a great lover of the past."

"I've always admired the portraits of Uncle Isaiah's uncle and aunt in the dining room."

"That's just it, he wanted Kekapuwai and Wahine-pio to hang with Nahinu and Kalaniulu."

"I have a wonderful place in my new house to hang the portraits of Kekapuwai and Wahine-pio, when I get them home. Of course, there will probably have to be some restoration work done on the paintings, and I know just the man to do it."

"Holo malie, Charlie, go slow," Aunt Rhoda said in a half-whimper. "It would make me feel funny if those pictures left this house. They are yours, I know. Sister Emily means them to be yours, but I feel attached to them. Old people get attached to things. Don't take them away yet."

At this moment Lydia Smith appeared. Freshly bathed and groomed, she looked almost attractive in a blue silk shirtwaist dress. Her navy and white spectator pumps gave her added height that lent an unfamiliar grace to her usual squat, slippered appearance. "Care for a drink, Charles?" she said with an uncharacteristic jaunty air.

"I would," he said flatly, suppressing irritation.

She sauntered through the parlor and the large middle room furnished with expensive teak chairs and tables, clustered around the piano with its avian decorations, leaving a faint pleasant trail of eau de cologne behind her. Charles followed her immediately, excusing himself to Aunt Rhoda.

Lydia Smith whispered—no crevice of the great rooms seemed to her to be free from listening ears:

"Aunt Rhoda is sure Aunty will leave most of all she has to her friends and various charities. Awful, isn't it!" By the way Lydia spoke, it was impossible to suspect she was taunting.

They had taken their first drink without interruption when Lydia Smith began to pour out her repressed heart in a sudden gush of emotion:

"For fifteen years now, Aunt Emily has lived with us in this house—she and her Mary Souza! Mary has all the privileges imaginable—a real little spy, running to Aunt Emily with every last piece of gossip. Aunt Rhoda has been so patient—so wonderfully patient. Aunt Emily is so critical of everything—so terribly critical. Aunt Rhoda's cronies are not good enough for Aunt Emily. She mimics them and calls them names. Calls them all *peasants!* O, poor soul, upstairs suffering so—God forgive me! But it's so hard to keep one's tongue quiet when so much has happened!"

The tall glass-panelled china closets dominated the room. In the dividing protrusions leading into the music room, huge calabashes held up with olona nets hung from the cross beams. On ledges and in glass cupboards that were part of the structure of the protrusions, various stone objects of the neolithic past reposed. The portraits of the High

Chief Nahinu and his wife Kalaniulu hung on either side of the sideboard at the northwest end of the room.

"I don't know why she ever came to Maui to live—she hated it so. She was critical of everything—and that Mary Souza chiming in rudely to echo Aunt Emily's sentiments."

"Forgive me, Laura. Please forgive me." The groans harbored the words now; they were intrinsically one and the same with the sporadic but continual moaning that exuded from behind the closed doors of Emily Christensen's rooms.

"I want those paintings," Charles said abruptly while Lydia was pouring a second drink.

"Didn't Aunt Rhoda say anything to you?"

"She did." He took the whiskey neat and poured himself a glass of water from a pitcher which stood near the tray of liquor and glasses.

"I must take Aunt Rhoda her glass of sherry. Doctor's orders. She has two drinks of sherry a day."

"The paintings, Lydia!" He took her arm and held it firmly. "Where are those paintings, Lydia?"

She squirmed to free herself from the hold he had on her arm. "You talk to Aunt Rhoda about them! I have nothing to say!"

"The point is, you do have something to say!" Charles snapped, his patience gone now. "I know all about your plan to sell them to Aylett Smith for five hundred dollars apiece. You ought to be ashamed of yourself!"

Lydia's mouth curled into a tight round knob, resembling an English walnut. It relaxed, and her face fell apart and took on the look of repulsion at first, and then alarm.

"Mary Souza! Why, I've worked myself to the bone in this house!" Her eyes flashed now, and she exerted enormous control to keep her voice at a low pitch. "It's been, 'Yes, Aunt Rhoda—right away, Aunt Emily—in a moment, Aunt Rhoda'!" She began to sob softly. "I have had no life of my own—no life at all! Aunt Rhoda has never let me out of her sight from the day I first entered this house. I've been nothing but a slave!"

"That has nothing to do with the crumby thing you have let yourself stoop to doing, so far as those paintings are concerned. They are not your property, nor, in any legal sense, are they Aunt Rhoda's."

Lydia whimpered like a hungry puppy.

"You influenced Aunt Rhoda in taking on the feelings she has now about the paintings. You did for the sole reason of making a few bucks. Blind as she is, she would never know if the paintings were here or not, and you would make up a million excuses concerning their whereabouts if there were ever an occasion for Aunt Rhoda to want the paintings to be shown."

"I've been like a neglected stepchild in this family for all these years. 'Poor old Lydia,' people keep saying. 'Poor old Lydia.' This is what I've become—the human sacrifice who's kept these old women going for all these years. It's not fair, I tell you! Not fair!"

"The only decent thing left for you to do is to have those paintings brought in as soon as you can."

"My cousin Aylett has always been proud of the fact that he is an Aylett by blood. He's had such a hard time. We all have. You people don't know what it is to be poor—to be nobody. Aylett's made a lot of money lately. He offered to pay for the paintings, and I know he'd take good care of them."

"What are you two doing?" Aunt Rhoda's voice came through the rooms, a thin reedy sound, lending the air a plaintive nether quality.

"I'm fixing your sherry, Aunty. I'll be right in!"

One of the maids came into the dining room to prepare the table for dinner.

"Here, Martha, take this to Mrs. Nahinu," Lydia said as she handed the young woman a small silver tray with the sherry.

"Aylett has as much right to those paintings as you."

"For a cool thousand, eh, Lydia? What kind of con artist have you become?"

"He has the money, and he's willing to pay for them," Lydia spat.

"And I'm sure Aunt Rhoda would be delighted to hear about this."

"O, damn the lot of you!" Lydia said and left the room.

Charles put his jigger glass on the sideboard and shook his head. Like a threatening cloud the pent-up ugliness, the heavy sadness that lingered everywhere in the house as it waited for death to put an end to Aunt Emily's lingering cries, engulfed him.

I am taking time and energy to stay here, he thought. It would be sheer masochism to remain a moment longer than it would take for him to dress and get the seven-fifty-five plane in the morning. It was too late to leave now. There were no more flights out of Kahului today. He groaned inwardly that he would have to spend another night in this house.

Quietly he went to the library and called the island airways for a ticket on the seven-fifty-five flight in the morning. If necessary he would purchase extra seats to have the paintings carried in the cabin. It would not be safe to let them be shipped with the baggage—a detail he would settle at the airport in the morning. He decided before joining

Aunt Rhoda again to send Mary Souza out for brown wrapping paper. He would ask her to help him wrap the paintings after Aunt Rhoda had retired for the night.

In the parlor he found Lydia dabbing her tearful eyes with a large white handkerchief. Aunt Rhoda made slightly audible sounds—a cross between chirp and cluck—as though she were repeating a prayer to herself.

"I've made arrangements to leave in the morning," he announced. "I've asked Lydia for some avocadoes and mangoes, and some taro, to take home. She's going to have Francisco bring them around to the front porch tonight. I take the seven-fifty-five flight in the morning."

"Going so soon, Charlie?" Aunt Rhoda asked plaintively.

"I must. There is really not much sense in my hanging around any longer." He sat in a dingy, overstuffed chair. "I'm afraid, Aunt Rhoda, it would be wrong for me to leave the paintings. They are in a bad state. They very much need restoring. There is even a puka in one section of the portrait of the Chiefess."

"Au'we ka pilikia e," Aunt Rhoda wailed.

Charles remembered seeing this hole punched into the canvas by careless handling at one time or another when he'd been here to help celebrate Aunt Rhoda's ninetieth birthday two years before. "Much work needs to be done on the paintings if they are to be saved at all." He turned to Lydia. "Will you have them brought down, Lydia! I'll call Mary, if you like. She can give Francisco a hand."

"If they are in such a bad condition, Charlie, perhaps you *should* take them along before they are ruined. Emily was never too careful in the way she handled those pictures."

Aunt Rhoda had capitulated. He rejoiced silently while Lydia Smith sped from the room, red-eyed and petulant. "I'll tell Mary Souza, myself, to help Francisco bring in the paintings," she said at the door.

The audible result of Aunt Emily's suffering sounded again in the rooms downstairs.

"My poor sister," Aunt Rhoda said in a choking voice.

"I was a belle in my day!" He could hear again the splendid voice making the announcement from the verandah of her bungalow in Honolulu. "I guess that's what every fool woman tells her grandnephews. I went to all the Palace functions with your grandfather in beautiful gowns whipped up by Sister Laura and her seamstress. Your grandfather was quite an ornament in his uniform and plumed helmet!" Time and again, he had probed the old woman for details. She told much, but always, always, something in the fabric of remembering was deficient; it made a harsh linen instead of soft pliant silk of her memories. Even so, she had made a whole era live for him.

"Forgive me, Laura, please forgive me."

"Those pictures of the brandy drinkers," Aunt Rhoda said, and disturbed Charles' musings. "I think Sister Emily made up the story about their being such heavy drinkers. Now where did she ever get that idea!" Aunt Rhoda coughed, and it was like the rasping call of a night petrel. "She really despised our mother's parents—as though they weren't our flesh and blood at all! But somehow she got possession of their pictures after Mamma died. Mamma had always hung them in our old home up the street."

"Aunt Emily never did hang them in her house in Honolulu," Charlie said.

"I know that. Isaiah was very critical of her for that. He even said once, that she was ashamed of them and took the pictures only to keep them out of sight."

There were sounds in the hall. Lydia, one of the maids, old Francisco, and Mary Souza entered the parlor like a troupe of stagehands and set the large painted portraits side by side against the wall near the door. Lydia dismissed the servants and made her own departure as soon as they were out of sight. The imposing Hawaiian couple looked out from the paint and canvas with all the famed dignity of nineteenth century Hawaiians.

"They were very handsome people," Charles said.

"Too damned dressed up," Aunt Rhoda answered quickly. She spoke as though she could see the canvases plainly.

"But those were the costumes of their times," he said in their defense.

Aunt Rhoda seemed now to be in deep reflection to bring from dimming sources a choice fragment of memory. "What I never did like about the paintings," she said at last, "was the way the little boy—I guess he was an uncle of mine, the one who died young—the way he has his head resting in the lap of his father. So undignified! And that awful scarlet silk shirt he's wearing with the lace collar. A regular sissy! Hawaiians were great on spoiling their children. They still do—they're very indulgent. This is the one thing I never liked about those pictures."

To what extent had his aunt's childlessness caused her to have so quaint, yet strong, a feeling of criticism for the child in the painting? He had always thought the little boy with his head burrowed into his father's lap displayed a charming uniqueness—the kind of affectionate display between a father and his child which you almost never saw in the great works of European portraiture.

"That child should have been kept out of the picture," Aunt Rhoda continued. "And maybe the Chiefess could have worn fewer ostrich plumes when she sat for the Frenchman to paint her."

"I've always liked the ostrich plumes. They give the Chiefess a dashing look, as though she had visited Europe and had charmed an artist there into painting her portrait in a costume that suggested the eighteenth century. I want my children to enjoy these paintings, too. They will be thrilled to know that the little boy in the doeskin trousers and scarlet shirt was a great-uncle of theirs."

At this juncture, Lydia appeared in the doorway and announced that dinner was on the table. Charles took Aunt Rhoda into the dining room, saw that she was comfortably seated, and excused himself.

He went to the library and called Honey's Bar. When Aylett Smith came to the telephone, Charles explained that he was taking the ancestral portraits to Honolulu in the morning. He also informed Aylett that there was an excellent restorer and copyist in Honolulu, who could reproduce the originals for about the same price he would have paid Lydia for them. Aylett was surprised at Charles' candor and his generosity and thanked him profusely for the offer.

Aunt Rhoda's infirmities made it necessary for her to retire at an early hour. Shortly after dinner, when one of those awkward silences that fall between people who don't have much to say to one another had come between Aunt Rhoda, Charles, and Lydia Smith, the old woman said bluntly, "He hia moe, paha? Shouldn't I be going to sleep?"

Charles walked his great-aunt to the downstairs entrance hall from which she could easily enter her room, formerly Great-uncle Isaiah's law office.

"So, you are really leaving us in the morning, Charlie?" the old woman said.

"I'm afraid I must get back to Honolulu."

"Well, tell the folks all about things here. I know they will be anxious to hear about Sister Emily."

Without warning, the recurrent product of Emily Christensen's delirium had escaped the upstairs hall, and came floating down to the vestibule where Charles and Aunt Rhoda stood talking. With the chilling tones of a kanikau chant: "Laura, forgive me," moaned Aunt Emily.

The walls of his bedroom admitted the woeful pleadings of Aunt Emily, a veiled mist of sound. Was it not possible for the drugs to give longer periods of relief to the old woman? Was she so loath to give up her life to the dark emptiness of time that even drugs could not quiet her restive spirit? The street lights outside the windows now filtered a dim illumination into the room. The huge aglaia at the front entrance was riotously in bloom. Sound, sight, and smell entered his nerve, muscle, and brain cells with a cruel insistence. He could not sleep. He was troubled.

Now that he was in possession of the oil portraits, the photographs, and his great-grandfather's papers, he was ready to run: to flee the scene so saturated with his memories of childhood. Yes, he hated the old house, and, to some degree, he hated his great-aunts. Everything here seemed to produce in him a sustained feeling of rancor. The whole thing seemed such a waste!

So much of his life had been colored by Emily Christensen's being: her opinions, her demands. The very fact that she was extant had, in later years, instilled a kind of amorphous rage in Charles. He had been periodically thrust upon her as a child—an agent of consolation for a rich, aging, and lonely relative. Something in young Charles had made him attractive to the old woman. He was spirited and bad tempered he knew; for every opinion she had, he had had one of his own.

"You're a God-damned piss-ant," Aunt Emily had said numerous times, "but, by golly, you've got a little spunk. Not like some of your woman-chasing relatives!" The Newton men were, to the last man and boy, woman chasers. "They squandered their birthright on rotten hussies. I can point out any number of the bitches that your grandfather, and his brothers, kept. Catch-colts all over the place!"

But, in spite of these pontifications, mixed as they were with oddments of impiety, Charles could remember the mannish generosity of his great-aunt, and, in some matters, her wonderful sense of fair play. That was the thing about living. You saw, time and again, the good and the bad mixed in people—a fantastic dualism of spirit, that was held somehow in balance by the entanglement of both extremes.

Aunt Emily had agreed to pay for his music lessons. "Not a God-damned member of the family has yet learned the difference between E flat and a block of wood. Now God damn it, you be the first one to play a tune from notes." For several years Aunt Emily had sent a check regularly to the finest piano teacher in Honolulu, an act for which he would be eternally grateful since his piano playing had always brought him so much pleasure.

At times when he had wanted to end all contact with Aunt Emily (but only after he had really dished it out to the old girl), he would remember his semi-annual purchase of a wardrobe at McInerny's which came about through the kindness of Aunt Emily. "Go get yourself some riggin's, boy." The salty usages of the whaler had not been entirely eradicated from the speech of the old folks. Chuckling to himself, he would thank his great-aunt profusely, and tear down to McInerny's before the act of largesse could be rescinded.

And there were the years at college. Although she had strongly disapproved of his going to the East Coast to school ("It will cost too God-damned much—warm clothes and the like!"), she had generously contributed to his costs as a student. "Remember, Charles," she had written in one letter, "willful waste brings woeful want, so make the best of this three hundred dollar cashier's check I have inclosed." Without her help, his pursuit of knowledge would have been garnered with far more discomfort and sacrifice than he had experienced.

What good would it do to go and see her now? Back of his thought remained the stinging truth of his having not visited the sickroom once since his arrival. He had said to Mary Souza that he would "look in" on Aunt Emily after dinner. He had not. Was death so terrifying? Would the sight of the pale form under her moist sheets sicken him? Would Aunt Emily rise from her moaning, unconscious recumbency and issue a final gush of vituperation—her threnody perhaps—a final blast at the world, studded with familiar invectives? Was he so callow that he could not spare himself one moment of his fortunate and comfortable life to pay a last call of respect upon someone who was dying: someone who had been generous and, though in a bungling way, quite concerned about his development as a human being? What have I become? he asked himself with the sudden rise of a hot recriminatory sense of guilt. What am I?

A gust of wind stirred the topmost branches of the magnolia trees into movement which cast huge shadows across the windows of his bedroom. He had already risen from the large historic bed and was jimmying himself awkwardly into his dressing gown.

The nurse let him into Aunt Emily's bedroom. He walked slowly, almost sheepishly, to the edge of the big four-poster. In the emaciated groaning form under the white sheet there was very little left of the tall, spirited woman he had known. She had been harridan and lady, all mixed in a sturdy, almost Amazonian frame. The past and present had vied eternally for supremacy in her spirit. Harsh judging of people was mixed with a greatness of heart in Aunt Emily.

How sad that she had fought the tenacious, eternal battle within herself over her racial origins. She was really as good a Hawaiian as she was a haole. Both streams of culture, merging within the framework of her personality, had made Emily Aylett Christensen one of the most interesting products of Hawaii. Hundreds and hundreds would be aware of her passing: a Victorian Hawaiian, full of conscience and morality.

Her bony frame moved under the sheet, and again the pleading cry of contrition escaped her thin purple lips. The cry brought Mary Souza from her little alcove, formerly Uncle Isaiah's dressing room, to the bedside.

"You come see Aunty at lass, Chahly!"

He nodded his head and forced himself to keep the tears from escaping their imprisonment in his eyes. "Yes, Mary I come say goodby to Aunt Emily, bless her cantankerous old soul."

He left the room hurriedly, and walked back to his bedroom. His eyes were wet now with the flow of tears. He let them fall freely down and over the contours of his face.

Johnny Warm

I had often wondered why my father would be called—always in a humorous, somewhat blustering way—by the quaint name of Johnny Warm. Ordinarily he was called Jack, or simply, Johnnie; but older members of the family, or very close friends, would see him and sing out in the abrupt, personal, open way of islanders, from across the street or from the opposite end of a room, "Ho there, Johnny Warm!"—the calls coming quite unexpectedly, like the roar of a large wave when you have let your attention wander away for a moment as you sit at the seashore, or like a large decayed branch succumbing finally to disintegrating processes and crashing to the ground in the dead silence of a woodland.

My father, at these times, would blush a little, respond with a trace of bravado, but never annoyance—while I would feel removed from some mysterious but probably pleasurable enough little secret. I had asked him, from time to time, why certain people called him by that name. Although he was generally quite willing to answer any question I asked him, especially if it referred to the past, he seemed reluctant in this case to give me a clear satisfactory answer until that night, some years ago now, when we were camped on the beach at Mikilua.

"We were traveling in the coach—the big one my great-grandfather Mark Hull had brought out from England in 1863, two years before he died," my father began, with a swift incisive look into the far reaches of Mikilua Valley. "We were running away from another epidemic that had swept down upon Honolulu. This time it was cholera. In Chinatown people were dying by the score." Then, impulsively, he rose and went to the spot where our supplies were stashed to make himself a whiskey and soda.

We were camping under the stars in the dead of summer, and the heavens were brilliantly clear, the odors from the sea of particularly penetrating redolence. Frequently we came to Mikilua Beach to camp out on its elegant stretch of clean white sand. The lonely shores of this beautiful fringe at the far western end of Oahu lured my father with a siren's persistence. Every opportunity for a picnic or a short holiday my father seized upon as a reason for taking us on another visit to Mikilua. It was as though he were paying faithful and decorous court to a beautiful woman. In fact we had a perfectly usable and attractive beach house at Kawela Bay where, upon my mother's stern insistence, we spent longer holidays; but my father's heart was not at Kawela, ever—Mikilua Beach was his first and passionate love.

This was entirely understandable; for all during his youth, and two generations previously, his family had owned the entire valley of Mikilua, of which the beach was but a fringe: the southwest border of a holding of fourteen thousand acres.

"My grandmother had chosen to use the coach because she wanted to travel fast, and because she wanted us to be all together in one vehicle," my father said, after returning with his drink. "There were seven of us children, old Kalama—Grandma's serving woman—and Malia, who was my little brother Henry's nurse. Quite a gang, I assure you, and no one riding on the seats above. Grandma thought it was safer if we all rode inside the coach as we drove out of town. When we got into the country, it was darkening and a mist was falling. She had promised us older children we could sit on the top seats of the tally-ho once we were safely out of town. But that night the weather didn't allow us to enjoy this great privilege." He laughed. "It was one of the joys of our lives as kids to ride atop that damned coach!"

He then looked wistfully into the valley with its high bordering ridges and the long sweep of its flat central bottom lands that appeared in a vague mass under the starry brilliance of light cast down from space through marvelously clear skies. With this intense look he seemed to possess again some of the smells, the sounds, the irrepressible joys of childhood and youth that connected him poetically to a life the broad valley had once known.

"I shall never forget driving up to Uncle Willson's ranch house in the dawn light—my trousers soaked through, and my grandmother muttering in Hawaiian something quite unintelligible to her serving woman, Kalama, after Jackson Tallot had told her what had happened to me, sitting next to him on the driver's seat, just a short while before we arrived at Manulani. We went to Uncle Willson's first. I'll explain this later, but first let me tell you about Jackson.

"Jackson Tallot had driven us that night. Jackson was really the blacksmith at Mikilua in those days, but Grandma had sent especially for him to come into Apua with the great coach, the tally-ho, so that she could carry as many of us as possible in one vehicle. For some reason, she didn't trust old Pilipo Archer, the half-white, who usually drove the coach from Mikilua to town and back for the many guests that Uncle Edward used to invite to the ranch, and for some reason she felt that her own coachman, the little Irishman Higgins, was not up to the job. I'm sure I've told you about Higgins—the one who murdered his wife in 1903—he was hanged for it, you know. On that night he followed behind us in Grandma's surrey with some of the house servants." My father finished his drink, swirling the ice in the glass as though it could somehow magically increase the molecules of whiskey remaining. Then he went for another drink.

We were camped in the open for it seldom rained at Mikilua Beach during the months of summer. Except for the heavy fall of dew which gave the early mornings there a particularly uncomfortable chill, it was an ideal place to sleep, exposed to heaven and the crashing sound of waves breaking in their race to land on the fringe of reef a hundred or so yards from the shore.

"We owned all of this in those days," my father continued, savoring, with a few protracted sippings, the flavor of his fresh drink. "We owned it all, and some of the finest horses and cattle bred in the islands in the early days were produced right here on this land." He spoke this for what seemed to me like the ten-thousandth time. "It was a beautiful ranch. We had everything here—all the comforts you would want—and great flocks of guinea fowl, turkey and peacocks roaming the valley, free of danger. There were no mongoose here in those days to eat all the eggs or the young of ground-nesting birds. O, it was a sight to see the peacocks lingering in the shade of great mango or kukui trees—a great sight to see—or to watch—in the late evening, the turkeys going to roost in those thickly branched wili wili trees that grew plentifully throughout the valley. And all of those screeching guinea fowl! We would ride up on a covey and take them by surprise. In a minute, they'd all be in flight, screaming their bloody heads off."

"I've always wondered about the cries of the peacocks," I said, remembering the eerie screech of this gaudy bird from the small flock one of my great-uncles still kept at his present place of residence at another section on the island, which were the descendants of specimens he had brought originally from Mikilua after the ranch was sold.

"We got used to the screeching of the peacocks. I used to like to hear them, even at night. They were an important part of the life of the valley. I can't imagine the ranch having been the place it was without the peacocks parading and screeching."

And I cannot imagine my father being the person he was without this endlessly charming relationship he possessed within him for birds, dogs and horses. I laughed, and he laughed and stretched full length on the sand, resting now on one of his elbows.

"Boy! how we have wandered from my story. I always get sidetracked when I think about the ranch." My father chuckled, seeming for a moment to be amused at himself over the diversionary flight of talk about some of the more romantic aspects of the ranch, instead of keeping to the story of the ride in the great coach, which somehow connected with his acquisition of his quaint pet name. I had heard about the peacocks, peafowl, wild turkeys, and scolding coveys of speckled alarmist guinea hens all of my life. "I'll try to stay with my story of my getting the nickname you're so niele, so curious, about," he said with a taunting look, now relaxed from the effect of the whiskey.

"We left town in a great hurry that evening. It was dusk, and I remember so well how pink and grey the skies had been. Jackson drove that big coach hell for leather out of town by King Street. Remember, we were running from cholera, and we took the quickest route out of town. It was no fun in those days to see one of those epidemics fall upon us. People died by the score—especially the Chinese and poorer class Hawaiians. It was awful!"

A strained look, a passing note of melancholy, registered on my father's countenance. As quickly as he could he shed it. My father enjoyed sentimentality enormously but rigorously avoided showing his feelings of sentiment. I suppose that is why he had loitered for years before allowing himself to explain to me the meaning of Johnny Warm.

He began to speak again, and I turned to listen. I had averted my face to allow him his show of emotion, even though it had been swiftly scuttled. "Jackson took the horses—four matched chestnuts from a herd of Caters that were kept at Mikilua—right down King Street, and away we went. By God! he was an excellent driver. It was no wonder Grandma had sent for him to come in with the coach.

"Jackson was a huge man. He had run away from a Louisiana plantation where he had been a slave. This had happened in the first months of the Civil War. He was little more than a kid when this happened. Somehow, eventually, he landed in Honolulu. My grandfather found him, halfstarved, on the docks and took him home with him to Apua. In time he revealed his skill as a smithy, and that was that! He was sent out to Mikilua where Gunner Johnson, the big Swede I've told you about, was growing old and hankering to go back to San Francisco. Gunner Johnson was a big man, but Jackson towered above him. Six foot, five—and all bone and muscle! He had a great squarish head and arms the size of totem poles. A strange man—at times quiet as hell—and serious. Seemed to me, he was always holding in a great pain of some kind which he carefully guarded as a secret he wished to keep strictly to himself. This had given him an angry look. Scared as hell of him, we kids were, at first, but after we learned he was really gentle as a lamb and that his facial expression was only a mannerism, we used to all haunt the blacksmith shop whenever we came out to the ranch."

Automatically my father had tossed his right arm north, toward the mountains—as though he were actually pointing to the long-demolished stables and the smithy at Mikilua Ranch.

I had heard a great deal about Jackson Tallot over the years, but never at one time had my father or my great-uncles summoned a detailed biographical account of the ex-slave's life. His skills and his useful exhibitions of inordinate strength, his loyalty, and dependability were oftentimes introduced into the enchanted diverse stories of the famed ranch life; but my father was moved, for some reason, to tell me all he knew of Jackson's life that night on Mikilua Beach.

"Jackson drove like a demon that night! But his hands were steady and sure!—and what enormous hands they were! My grandmother kept calling to him in Hawaiian to take care of the horses. 'Nana ika lio! Look out for those horses!' Horses were her pride. She loved them like no other woman I have ever known. And she was a great rider—her seat was perfect. She rode astride even in those days. But she needed to have no fears that night. So long as Jackson was at the reins the horses would be perfectly driven.

"Some of the dogs had followed us that night—the greyhounds from Apua, and your Uncle Beaufort's wolfhound, Boris. Jackson thought Grandma had said ilio, which means dog, and he had kept singing out in his deep voice, 'No fee-ah, Ma'am, dem dawgs is doin' fine!' 'Dogs be damned,'—or something of the sort—my grandmother had barked. 'I'm talking about the horses! Nana ika lio—nana ika lio!' she kept calling out.

"We took the road up to Halemano at a good clip. We were heading for Manulani, your Great-uncle Willson's ranch, where the race horses were bred. Grandma had planned for us to spend the night there and then head back to Ewa the next day and home to Mikilua. I don't know why we didn't just stay on at Manulani for Uncle Willson and Aunt Elizabeth had plenty of room. But your Great-grandmother Kaloka was a peculiar woman. She didn't much like your Aunt Elizabeth. I think it was because Aunt Elizabeth was so quiet and aloof. She was educated in England—always reading a book, or playing on the piano."

My father's habit of wandering over vast landscapes of subject matter whenever he told a story was a bit irksome, yet, actually, I enjoyed this, for he unwittingly packed his stories—mostly reminiscences of his charmed youth in Hawaii of the eighties and nineties—with rich and stunning details which he might never have mentioned at all had he consciously put more order and pattern into his storytelling. Some of these details were far more interesting to me than the little "plots" or the "point," as it is sometimes expressed, of his conversationally rendered tales. His romantic turn of mind made him dwell on fascinating impedimenta like his recollection of festooning the horses with flower leis and strands of green maile vines when they went on riding excursions. In remembering his early childhood days at the house at Apua he recalled things like the fine iron fence that surrounded the large property, the strange thin tall and silent Eurasian butler, Chang, and the poignant cries of families passing the house, as they took relatives afflicted with leprosy to the docks from which they were sent to Kalaupapa, that desolate corner of the islands.

My father had gone for his third drink, and I had let my fancy call up the stunning impressionism of his recollections. When he returned I made mention of my thoughts and he chuckled, but said nothing until he began again to launch into his story of the ride to Manulani in the great coach.

"O, what a night that was! It was windy as hell—and when we reached Kipapa it had begun to rain. Grandma ordered the coach stopped so we could all take care of physical necessities—in the rain, of course. We were seven children, Grandma, Kalama, and little Henry's nurse, in the tally-ho. The others followed in the surrey and a wagonette—a mile or so behind us now. For some reason, I was unable to relieve myself, although I wanted like hell to pee. 'Go ahead, Keoni, go ahead, Johnnie! Do your business like a good boy,' Grandma had said. 'I can't, Kuku, I can't!' I had answered—and then put up a hell of a howl! 'Keko!' Grandma had snapped, calling me a monkey in Hawaiian.

"When Jackson had returned to the coach and saw that I was bellowing (a term my father constantly used to denote crying) he asked Grandmother to let me sit with him in the driver's seat. This put a stop to my bellowing for after a moment of resistance my grandmother consented, and asked that one of the oilskin coats be dragged from the box under the driver's seat for me to use since it was still raining. After wrapping me into this, Jackson, with a single powerful thrust, lifted me smack into the driver's seat atop the coach. We drove on at a canter—the chestnuts were pretty fired up by now and wanted to pull into a full gallop! Not with Jackson at the reins, though. Not while those big powerful hands held them.

"'You take care of those horses!' Grandma had said to Jackson before we pulled off again. 'Those animals are my husband's pride and joy—and mine, too!' 'Yessum, yessum!' Jackson had answered with a smile. He realized now that she had been talking about the horses, and not the dogs, when she had called to him from the coach way back at Waiau.

"'Your granny shore do love ha hahses! Man ah-lahve, she love 'em moah en she love ha own chillun!' Jackson had said as we were climbing the Kipapa rise."

I let my thoughts dwell on the smithy at Mikilua, as my father fell into a period of silence, toying again with his drink. I had heard always, it seemed to me, scattered fragments about Jackson Tallot. There had been talk of his killing the plantation overseer; and of his having thrown a man overboard, on the whaling ship which had brought him into the Port of Honolulu, who had called him a God-damned run-away nigger. And my great-grandfather used to love to tell the story of finding the young giant down on the waterfront, half-starved and desperate—beached in Honolulu because of the incident at sea, which had almost cost the life of a namecalling sailor. When my father began to talk again, his face lighted up. In the starlight, he seemed to be smiling.

"We drove along at a good clip, heading into Wahiawa, Jackson talking a blue streak, which was funny, because ordinarily he talked damned little. 'Thim dawgs is guine a run unner dim wheels one o' dese times, shoise mah name's Tallot! Thut big Roosian fellah de woist of da lot da way he run lak grease laightnin' frum one side t'other.'"

Father mimicked the giant plausibly, which was surprising to me, because islanders before radio and television seldom heard the speech of Southerners.

"It was a night I shall never forget!" My father had started to talk again after another brief pause; but at this point, a falling star interrupted my father's monologue. We both fell silent and watched its flickering descent. "Funny damned things, aren't they?"

I agreed with a slight nod, resenting the intrusion. Somehow I could not concern myself, on that night, with the always mystifying and gripping phenomena of a disintegrating planet's fall through the darkened heavens. In a few moments my father obligingly continued his story:

"Now, what I wanted was to ask Jackson about the welts on his back. We had heard talk among the big folks that Jackson bore the evil marks of his slavery in the form of six great scars that ran diagonally across his back. We children had been told never to question Jackson about this matter. He was very sensitive, they said, about those scars, and I can't say as I much blame the man for having felt that way.

"He could do anything, that man could! He learned cowpunching and rode among the klu bushes and cactus in the Mikilua hills with the rest of the paniolas. He could kill and slaughter pipi (cattle) with the best of them. In later years Uncle Christopher taught him a lot about horse-breeding and the care of Thoroughbreds. He was the best all round man they ever had at Mikilua! Look at that, boy, another falling star! Damned things give me an eerie feeling!"

My mind was far from astronomical matters that night. The Milky Way itself could have sent down a coruscant shower of planetary sequins, and it would not have diverted my thoughts from my father's telling of the incident in his and Jackson Tallot's lives. Lady, one of our three setters, had come over to sit at my feet, and, after sending me a long doleful look characteristic of her breed, she had settled quickly into another indolent snooze with her head resting on my ankles.

"Jackson told me things that night he had never told anyone since he had come to Hawaii. He told me about his father and mother—funny! It had been hard to imagine he might have had parents. And about life on the plantation he fled from—and about New Orleans and life on the river. 'Boy,' he said, 'those was dahk times foh ole Jackson!' It must have been difficult for a young man of his spirit to take the slave life easily! He told me about voodoo queens and Cajun farmers, about the great creole mansions and the families who lived in them. It was really like a story from some famous book. All the while he talked, he had driven those horses as smoothly as though he were driving the Queen of England to church. His driving was so smooth and controlled it lulled Grandma and the others in the coach to sleep. There had not been a peep out of any of them for miles.

"After we had passed through Wahiawa and were driving on the Manulani road, I had the worst urge to pee. It was cold and drizzly now, and, if it weren't for Jackson's talking, I would have fallen asleep a long time before." My father had begun to laugh when he reached this point in his narrative. "When I told Jackson that I wanted to pee in the worst way, he had laughed like a hyena.

"'Boy, you jist do it in yo paints, now. Ah ain' a gonna stop for de woild. If ah deed, yoh granny skin us both ah-lahve!' Then he had laughed! He had laughed like I had never seen him laugh before.

'Yaw'll beddah do it rahight in yoh paints. Yoh say, yoh cold, boy, well, dis is da bess way now foh yoh'll ta keep warm. Do it in yoh paints, an Ah'll call you Johnny Warm from now on!'"

"Why have you never told me this before?" I asked with a degree of petulance.

"There is always a time and place to tell things, boy. I have so many things to tell about my youth, I hope I live long enough to tell them all to you. Johnny Warm! The name has stuck with me all these years!"

"I will tell Miu Lan Chong, my classmate, about this when school starts again," I said tauntingly. "She always likes to hear tales about her grandfather."

Then a great silence had fallen between us. Even the night and the sea seemed to have held in abeyance their particular life of sounds.

"Did you ever ask Jackson about the welts on his back, Papa?" I said finally.

"Jackson did show me the welts on his back one day—right here at Mikilua. We had become great friends after that ride, and one day I asked him about his scars. He always kept a shirt on even during the hottest days as he stood at the forge. I realized then why he had been so touchy about those scars over the years, because he wept like I have seen no man weep when he tore off his shirt so I could see."

Then, after what seemed an inordinate period of silence, my father said abruptly: "It's time we turned in, boy! Everybody is asleep!"

Design and typesetting by ParaGraphics, Inc., Bloomfield, NJ
Printing and binding by Thomson-Shore, Inc., Dexter, MI